The wistful, almost yearning expression on Ryan's handsome face as she'd held baby Georgina had confused her.

Then it was back to the coldness in his blue eyes and the hard set to his jaw that she'd grown used to over the past six months as she'd pressed for more to be done in bringing her cousin's murderer to justice.

"If you hadn't been here, Meghan, I would have been able to control the situation."

His saying the words aloud felt like a phy[...] Georgina's life hung in the balance. Beca[...] squeezed her eyes tight. "Please, dear Lo[...] Georgina safe. Please let us find her."

When she opened her eyes, she found Rya[...] with an arrested look on his face.

"Why is the missing baby so important to y[...] asked.

An ambulance roared to a halt a few feet away, saving her from answering.

But soon she'd have to tell him.

Books by Terri Reed

Love Inspired Suspense

Strictly Confidential
*Double Deception
Beloved Enemy
Her Christmas Protector
*Double Jeopardy
*Double Cross
*Double Threat Christmas
Her Last Chance
Chasing Shadows
Covert Pursuit
Holiday Havoc
  "Yuletide Sanctuary"
Daughter of Texas
†*The Innocent Witness*
†*The Secret Heiress*
The Deputy's Duty

Love Inspired

Love Comes Home
A Sheltering Love
A Sheltering Heart
A Time of Hope
Giving Thanks for Baby
Treasure Creek Dad

*The McClains
†Protection Specialists

TERRI REED

At an early age Terri Reed discovered the wonderful world of fiction and declared she would one day write a book. Now she is fulfilling that dream and enjoys writing for Love Inspired Books. Her second book, *A Sheltering Love,* was a 2006 RITA® Award finalist and a 2005 National Readers' Choice Award finalist. Her book *Strictly Confidential,* book five in the Faith at the Crossroads continuity series, took third place in the 2007 American Christian Fiction Writers Book of the Year Award, and *Her Christmas Protector* took third place in 2008. She is an active member of both Romance Writers of America and American Christian Fiction Writers. She resides in the Pacific Northwest with her college-sweetheart husband, two wonderful children and an array of critters. When not writing, she enjoys spending time with her family and friends, gardening and playing with her dogs.

You can write to Terri at P.O. Box 19555, Portland, OR 97280. Visit her on the web at www.loveinspiredauthors.com, leave comments on her blog, www.ladiesofsuspense.blogspot.com, or email her at terrireed@sterling.net.

THE DEPUTY'S DUTY

TERRI REED

Love Inspired

If you purchased this book without a cover you should be aware that this book is stolen property. It was reported as "unsold and destroyed" to the publisher, and neither the author nor the publisher has received any payment for this "stripped book."

Special thanks and acknowledgment to Terri Reed for her contribution to the Fitzgerald Bay miniseries.

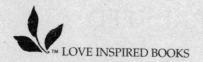

™ LOVE INSPIRED BOOKS

Recycling programs for this product may not exist in your area.

ISBN-13: 978-0-373-67514-2

THE DEPUTY'S DUTY

Copyright © 2012 by Harlequin Books S.A.

All rights reserved. Except for use in any review, the reproduction or utilization of this work in whole or in part in any form by any electronic, mechanical or other means, now known or hereafter invented, including xerography, photocopying and recording, or in any information storage or retrieval system, is forbidden without the written permission of the editorial office, Love Inspired Books, 233 Broadway, New York, NY 10279 U.S.A.

This is a work of fiction. Names, characters, places and incidents are either the product of the author's imagination or are used fictitiously, and any resemblance to actual persons, living or dead, business establishments, events or locales is entirely coincidental.

This edition published by arrangement with Love Inspired Books.

® and TM are trademarks of Love Inspired Books, used under license. Trademarks indicated with ® are registered in the United States Patent and Trademark Office, the Canadian Trade Marks Office and in other countries.

www.LoveInspiredBooks.com

Printed in U.S.A.

Bear with each other and forgive one another
if any of you has a grievance against someone.
Forgive as the Lord forgave you.
—*Colossians* 3:13

Writing a continuity series involves the collaborated efforts of the other authors and the editors. It was a joy to work with my fellow authors: Shirlee McCoy, Valerie Hansen, Rachelle McCalla, Stephanie Newton and Lynette Eason. I'd like to thank my editors Emily Rodmell and Tina James for your patience, for the time and energy you put into making all our books the best they can be.

ONE

"The house is the second one on the right."

Deputy Chief Ryan Fitzgerald nodded to the officer sitting next to him and tightened his grip on the steering wheel of the official Fitzgerald Bay vehicle. He pulled to the curb in front of a boxy house with a front brick facade and white siding. The paved driveway was empty. He doubted this trip to the town of Revere would pay off, but it was the only lead he had to a murder suspect and a missing eighteen-month-old little girl.

He glanced around, taking stock of the neighborhood. Quiet, tree-lined street. No one was out and about on this blistering June day. Better indoors, out of the sun and the humidity. The lucky ones with air conditioners, blowing out cool air.

His gaze snagged on a burgundy Subaru parked across the street. His gut clenched.

Meghan Henry's car.

What was the nosy reporter doing here? Ever since she had arrived in Fitzgerald Bay six months ago, she'd been hounding him for answers in her cousin Olivia Henry's murder. He didn't blame her for wanting to see justice done. Olivia's death had rocked the community of Fitzgerald Bay and the Fitzgerald family. She'd been his brother Charles's nanny for his twins at the time of her death. Everyone who knew her had said she was a sweet woman. No one could understand why someone would kill her.

Her body had been discovered at the base of the lighthouse cliffs. A life cut too short.

So yes, Ryan understood Meghan's desire to see the culprit arrested and put away, but not at the expense of his family.

With everyone in town believing Charles was capable of killing Olivia Henry, all of the Fitzgerald Bay police force had worked overtime to clear his name. Meghan Henry's constant questions and snooping had hindered the investigation and inflamed the citizens of Fitzgerald Bay with suspicion.

And now here she was, poking around at the one lead he had to go on in another recent murder case.

Burke Hennessy, a prominent lawyer in town, had been found dead in his home by his wife, Christina. At first glance the death appeared accidental or possible suicide. But the M.E. discovered evidence to suggest murder. And his wife was the prime suspect.

Burke had been running for the mayoral seat until his untimely death. The medical examiner found Burke had ingested a potent combination of drugs, enough to incapacitate him while the murderer suffocated him with a down pillow. Feathers had been found in his nose and throat and the official cause of death had been ruled asphyxiation. They found the pillow that had been used hidden in a closet in the Hennessy home. Christina's fingerprints were all over it. The D.A. thought he had a good case for murder. Now all Ryan had to do was find Christina and bring her into custody.

If Meghan hadn't already spooked Christina and sent her fleeing again.

Ryan was going to arrest Meghan for obstructing justice the second he saw her. He could imagine her wrinkling up her pert nose and daring him with her green-hued hazel eyes. The woman possessed a fiery spirit, for sure. A testament to her Irish heritage.

Like his sisters and mother.

"Stay with the car," Ryan said to the rookie in the passenger seat as he exited the vehicle. "Keep an eye out for anything suspicious."

Officer Jackson nodded and climbed out to rest his lanky frame against the fender. He crossed his arms over his chest.

Ryan marched up the concrete steps and rapped his knuckles on the heavy-duty metal screen door.

From somewhere inside a woman sang a lullaby, the sound melodic and pleasing. And familiar. He paused, searching his brain for recollection.

A second later a woman, mid-forties with frosted hair and an ample girth, appeared at the door. Since the Hennessys lived a few doors down from Ryan's family home, he recognized Helen Yorke, the Hennessys' former housekeeper.

Helen wiped her hands on an apron covered with red cherries as her brown eyes widened with surprise. She pushed open the screen door. "Deputy Chief Fitzgerald?"

"Hello, Helen," Ryan responded, trying to peer into the house over the woman's shoulder. "Is Christina Hennessy here?"

She shook her head. "Not at the moment. Why?"

Not a wild-goose chase after all. Things were looking up. When his youngest sister, Keira, a rookie officer with the FBPD, had suggested contacting the Hennessys' ex-housekeeper, Ryan had been dubious. He couldn't see Christina seeking refuge with a former employee. Looked like he owed Keira an apology for doubting her. And a chocolate sundae. His baby sis had a penchant for chocolate.

"Do you know where Mrs. Hennessy went? Did she have Georgina with her?" Ryan asked, keeping a sharp eye out for any sign of deception in the woman's face and demeanor.

"Christina showed up on my doorstep yesterday asking if I could keep little Georgina for a few days while she dealt with some personal business. She was so distraught over the death of poor Burke I could hardly refuse. What is this about, Deputy?"

Distraught, my eye, Ryan thought, but refrained from commenting. "Georgina is here, then." This, at least, was good news. The child was safe. When Christina had disappeared with her adoptive daughter, Ryan had feared for the little girl's safety.

Helen tucked in her chin. "She's in the other room. We were putting her down for a nap."

We. *Meghan.* Anger churned in Ryan's gut.

"Meghan Henry is here, then." He needed the confirmation. At Helen's nod, he asked, "How do you know Miss Henry?"

"We became friendly last January when she arrived in Fitzgerald Bay after her poor cousin was murdered. She'd been very supportive when I had to leave the Hennessys' employ to take care of my mother. Meghan stopped by today to see how I was doing. Wasn't that sweet of her?"

"Yes, very," Ryan agreed, because he'd been raised to be polite. Sweet had nothing to do with it. Meghan was chasing a story. Burke Hennessy's death was big news. The fact that he'd been murdered hadn't been released to the public yet. So how had she heard that Christina was the prime suspect so quickly? "Excuse me a moment."

Ryan jogged back to Jackson. "Call Dispatch. Tell them we have a bead on Christina Hennessy and need to stake out this address. Also, notify Child Protective Services that we are removing Georgina Hennessy from her current location."

Jackson nodded and moved to do as asked. Ryan returned to the front door of Helen Yorke's house.

Helen frowned, her gaze going to Jackson by the Fitzgerald Bay police vehicle. "What's going on, Deputy?"

He glanced up and down the deserted street. When would Christina return? Better to remove the child before any confrontation. "I am taking Georgina Hennessy into protective custody."

Helen's gaze snapped back to him and widened. "Custody?"

"May I come in?"

The woman blinked. "Not until you tell me what's going on."

Appreciating her protectiveness of Georgina, Ryan said, "It would be better if I explained to you inside."

She hesitated then stepped back. "Excuse the mess. My mother passed on and I've been trying to box up her things to get the house ready to sell."

Entering the home, Ryan mentally catalogued the interior. Taped boxes stacked in the corner.

Half-full boxes littered the area rug over scarred hardwood floors. Three arched doorways led to other rooms and a hall opened to the left.

However, Meghan Henry was not in view. She must be with the child.

Helen set her hands on her hips and gave him a pointed look.

"Mrs. Hennessy is a suspect in her husband's murder," Ryan stated.

Shock flooded the older woman's expression. "What?" Helen shook her head. "No. Christina loved Burke."

"We have evidence implicating her. But for now I'm taking Georgina into custody," Ryan explained. "To protect her."

Doubt clouded Helen eyes. "You're sure of this?"

"It's still early in the investigation." He played on her maternal instincts. "The child's safety must be a priority. If Christina is innocent, she'll regain custody of her daughter quickly enough."

Placing her hand over her heart, Helen said, "Poor Georgina. Follow me."

Ryan made a quick walk-through of the kitchen, dining room and a bedroom, verifying Christina wasn't on the premises before joining Helen outside a room at the end of the hall.

As Ryan approached, she said, "I'll pack a couple of bottles and some finger food. She'll be hungry soon."

He allowed her to pass. When he entered the small bedroom, he halted abruptly. Meghan Henry cradled the sleepy toddler in her arms as she sang. The sound of her voice and the sight of her cuddling the child wrapped around Ryan's senses. His chest tightened.

Meghan bent close to coo as she bounced the sleepy little one in her arms. The red dress she wore heightened the color of her cheeks. Tenderness softened the brackets that had pinched the corners of her mouth the last time he'd seen her—when she'd stormed into his office demanding to know what he was doing to solve her cousin's murder. The love shining in Meghan's hazel eyes was unmistakable. And curious.

The sight unexpectedly touched something deep inside Ryan.

Seeing this softer, calmer side of Meghan appealed to him on an elemental level—which set his teeth on edge. He didn't understand why the sight of her holding a baby would make his insides melt and his heart ache.

He'd been there in the hospital when his nephew Sean was born. Watched his sister Fiona care for her newborn boy, heard her make the identical cooing sounds that were now emanating from Meghan. He'd witnessed plenty of women attending to children of various ages. But he hadn't felt this same strange expanding pressure building in his chest.

He softly cleared his throat to announce his presence as much as to release the tension knotting his shoulders.

Meghan glanced up. There was no surprise or repentance in her tear-filled eyes. The gentle smile curving her lips hit him in the solar plexus like the business end of a nightstick.

His mouth went dry. *Whoa, buster. Don't go losing perspective because of this woman.*

He drew in air and forced himself to push back the warmth burrowing deep inside him.

"What are you doing here?" he asked, careful to keep his voice low so as not to upset the toddler who stared at him with bright blue eyes.

"Following a lead the same as you," Meghan replied in a soft tone.

Frustration roped a knot in his chest. "You're interfering in my investigation. If you had a lead, you should have come to me."

She arched an eyebrow. Distrust oozed off her in waves.

That rankled. "What do you know?"

"I know Christina and Burke Hennessy weren't the upstanding citizens everyone believed them to be," she said.

He frowned. It was no secret that there was little love lost between the Hennessys and the Fitzgeralds. Burke Hennessy had been a prideful bully but there'd never been any hint of illegal activity associated with the lawyer and his socialite wife. So what would have led Meghan to make such a judgment? Had she uncovered information critical to his case? "If you know something that will help in my investigation into Burke Hennessy's death, you'd better tell me."

"Keep your voice down," she instructed with a pointed look at the toddler in her arms now squirming to be set free.

Reining in his frustration, he forced himself to let the questions go. There would be time enough for that later. "I'm taking Georgina into protective custody."

In a low voice, she asked, "So you do think Christina's responsible for her husband's death?"

"I do."

She nodded as if satisfied with his answer. "Do you have a car seat?"

His stomach sank. He hadn't expected to find Christina much less the toddler. "No."

"I do. So I guess we'll be taking my car."

She'd come prepared. Why? The question hovered on the tip of his tongue, but a strange sense of urgency tingled at the base of Ryan's neck. Pushing back his need for answers, he said, "We need to go."

"No one's going anywhere!" A woman's nasal voice invaded the room.

Meghan let out a gasp of alarm.

Ryan whipped around and found Christina Hennessy filling the doorway. The once-polished socialite now looked harried—her usually perfect blond hair mussed and her slacks and blouse wrinkled as if she hadn't changed clothes in several days. An almost wild fervor glittered in her green eyes setting off alarm bells in Ryan's head.

But the .38 revolver she held aimed at Meghan froze his blood.

A woman on the edge with a gun. A bad combination.

Beside her stood a muscle-bound thug with a nasty-looking scar running down the side of his face.

Anger directed mostly at himself shuddered through Ryan. He'd been so distracted by Meghan and the ridiculous soft emotions she had inspired that he'd let his guard down. He hadn't heard danger approaching. His instincts had kicked in too late.

His skills were rusty. Too much time spent at a desk and not out in the field.

Where was Jackson? Ryan could only hope the rookie wasn't lying dead outside.

Time to take control. Rapidly assessing the situation, he decided the best option was to keep everyone calm and his service weapon holstered. The quarters were too tight, the chances of someone getting hurt too great. He'd have a better opportunity of disarming Christina and dealing with her thug outside.

He slowly raised his hands in entreaty as he stepped in Christina's line of sight. Hopefully, he provided an effective shield for Meghan and the toddler. "Let's stay calm and talk about this."

"Give me the kid!" Christina demanded, gesturing the gun with jerky movements.

"No one's giving anyone anything." *Except for when you give me that gun.*

Ryan's heart hammered in his chest. Fear that she might accidently shoot one of them squeezed his lungs. He forced himself to remain calm, to sound composed. "Put down the gun, Mrs. Hennessy."

Her lips drew back, baring sharp white teeth. "You're a Fitzgerald. What are you doing here?"

"We were worried about Georgina." Ryan eased forward a step.

Christina stepped to the side. "She's fine. We're all fine."

Ryan mirrored her move. "Mrs. Hennessy, we need you to come in to the station house. We have some questions to ask you about Burke's death."

She frowned. "I've answered all your questions. I'm the one who found him."

There was something decidedly off about this woman. Ryan knew he wasn't dealing with a rational person. Best to appease her and keep this from turning into a deadly situation. "Yes, you did. We have just a few more things to clear up. Then you and Georgina can be reunited."

Christina jerked slightly. "Move out of the way," she cried. "I want the baby."

Odd how she kept referring to Georgina in such a distant manner. Not sure what to make of it, Ryan glanced at Meghan holding the now fussy toddler.

"Fine," Ryan said, keeping his voice low and composed. "We can all move into the living room, okay? It's a little cramped in here."

Instead of retreating, Christina moved fully into the small bedroom. The thug hovered near the door, blocking them in.

"Out," Christina said, motioning wildly with the gun.

A fresh wave of alarm that she'd discharge a stray shot rammed through him. He had to get Meghan and the toddler out safely. Keeping his arms wide and moving slowly, he reached his hand back. "Meghan, come here."

Shifting the eighteen-month-old onto her hip, she eased toward him, slipped her hand into his and held on tight. Making sure he stayed consistently between Meghan clutching the baby and the madwoman with the gun, he moved them toward the door.

"Tell Muscles here to get out of the way," he instructed.

The thug made a threatening growl low in his throat.

Christina snorted. "Go on, Jay. Lead them out."

With a scowl, Jay led them back down the hall. Ryan positioned Meghan and Georgina in front of him and hustled them toward the living room. Christina filed in behind Ryan, ramming the muzzle of the gun sharply into his kidneys.

For a second he contemplated disarming the woman now, but if she got off a shot and missed him, the bullet could hit Meghan or the baby. A risk he wasn't willing to take. He had to be patient. There would be a moment to strike.

He leaned in close to Meghan and whispered, "Be ready. Protect the baby."

Her honey-blond hair tickled his cheek as she nodded.

In the living room, Jay barred the exit with his massive frame.

Helen Yorke lay in an unconscious heap on the floor. Horror shot through him. He sent up a silent plea, praying she wasn't dead. He didn't want anyone's death on his conscience.

Georgina let out an unhappy wail.

Meghan made a distressed sound at the sight of Helen. "What did you do to her?"

Christina cackled, an unhinged sound that raised the fine hairs at the back of Ryan's neck.

"She'll be fine. Jay has his uses." Christina attempted to step around Ryan toward Meghan, and Ryan could see Helen begin to stir. "Give me the child."

Noting that Christina's finger wasn't on the trigger, Ryan seized the opportunity. He grabbed hold of the gun but also Christina's hand and swung her away from Meghan.

Christina's hold on the gun slipped. The revolver clattered to the floor and slid across the hardwood out of sight beneath the aged leather couch.

"Owwww," Christina screamed in fury. "Jay!"

A roar echoed in the small house, arising from Jay's barreled chest.

Meghan cried out a warning. "Ryan, watch out."

Ryan pivoted. Too late. Jay jumped on Ryan's back before he could get to his own holstered weapon.

Jay's bulk drove Ryan forward. Pain shot up Ryan's leg as his left ankle buckled. He hit the floor with a smack to his knees and nearly collapsed beneath Jay's gorilla-size weight.

His injuries making him want to do a little roaring of his own, Ryan instead gritted his teeth and grappled with the thug, trying to gain the advantage. Ryan drove his head back into Jay's pectoral muscle and thrust his hip up, creating an angle. Jay's beefy fists cracked across Ryan's ribs with painful impact. Ignoring the jarring hits, Ryan continued with the move, driving his hips across Jay and flipping him over.

Ryan wrapped his legs around Jay and yanked him down while hooking his forearms around Jay's neck and squeezing.

Just as he'd thought. Gym muscles. All show, no go. It took a lifetime of grappling with three brothers to make a man a real fighter.

Georgina's frantic cries bounced off the walls.

From his peripheral vision, Ryan saw Christina scrambling to recover her weapon from beneath the couch.

"Meghan, run!" he yelled.

Disregarding his directive, Meghan handed the screaming toddler to a now conscious Helen. Meghan launched herself at Christina and knocked her aside. The woman went flying on her backside and slid to a stop. Her beige slacks hitched to her knees. A cream-colored sock sagged at her ankles. Her brown loafers had dirt on the bottom.

In her hands, she held the gun. "Not another step!" she screamed at Meghan.

Meghan halted, skidding in her heeled sandals on the hardwood.

Christina jumped to her feet and yanked Georgina from Helen's arms.

Keeping the revolver aimed at Meghan, Christina said, "Deputy Fitzgerald, let Jay go or your friend here dies."

"Christina, no," Helen pleaded. "Don't do this."

"Shut up!" Christina swung the gun in Helen's direction.

Helen cowered away.

Ryan's gaze locked with Meghan. The panic in her eyes seared him. The situation had gone horribly out of his control. And it was his fault. Frustration clawed like a hungry lion through his veins. For a second he tightened his hold on Jay, wanting nothing more than to finish what he'd started.

But doing so jeopardized everyone in the room.

Abruptly Ryan released him.

The big man scuttled to his feet and then landed a vicious kick to Ryan's side. Pain zinged through him.

With helpless rage, he watched Christina Hennessy and her henchman head out the door with Georgina. He yanked out his phone and dialed 9–1–1.

Meghan launched herself at Christina with a ferocious yell. "You can't take her!"

Jay backhanded Meghan, sending her flying to the floor.

Fury propelled Ryan to his feet. His ankle gave

out and he stumbled. The phone flew from his hand and landed with a clatter against the floor. Jay took off.

Meghan scrambled for the phone. She found it and then rushed to Ryan's side as he painfully hauled himself to his knees. She offered her shoulder as support, wrapping her arm around his waist and helped him to his feet. His torso was on fire. Most likely a cracked rib.

A dark bruise marred Meghan's fear-filled face, making him feel worse than the blows he'd suffered.

"Stay here!" Untangling himself from her, he hobbled out the door.

A black sedan disappeared around the corner with tires squealing. Automatically, he noted the license plate number.

At the curb an unconscious Jackson lay crumpled on the ground beside the front wheel well of his vehicle, blood covering his face. Fearing for the young officer, Ryan limped to his side and bent to check his pulse. He was alive. Unsure of the extent of Jackson's injuries, Ryan didn't want to do any more damage by attempting to move him.

He hobbled to the back of the vehicle, noting that all of the tires had been slashed, and grabbed the first-aid kit.

Rage pounded at Ryan's temples in rhythm to

the throbbing in his ankle and side. He pressed a wad of gauze to Jackson's wound.

Self-recriminations swamped Ryan. He'd made an utter mess of things. Christina had escaped with Georgina. Jackson was down. The car was useless.

He was a cop, knew the importance of being proactive and vigilant. And had always lived up to that responsibility, regardless of the cost. He'd sacrificed a friendship to protect an innocent person. He'd done the right thing.

He'd never forgive himself if anything happened to the little girl because he'd failed to stop Christina and her thug, thus putting Georgina in danger.

Meghan came hurrying out, his phone pressed to her ear. She skidded to a halt, her heeled sandals sliding on the sidewalk. She handed him the phone. "Nine-one-one."

After identifying himself, he explained the situation and gave the license plate number of Christina's getaway car. The dispatcher assured him the local patrol officers would respond immediately and an ambulance was on its way.

"We'll need two," he said before hanging up.

Helen staggered out of the house. Despite her own knock to the head, when she spotted Jackson, her mothering instincts sent her straight to him. Leaving Ryan leaning against the side of his vehicle, Meghan rushed to help Helen to sit on the curb next to Jackson.

Ryan slammed his palm against the hood of his vehicle then wobbled. Every second he stood there Christina and her goon were getting farther away. His gaze grazed over Meghan's car and the temptation to pursue the perps grabbed ahold of him and squeezed. He fought the instinct; the last thing he needed to do was leave the scene of a crime. He had an officer down and a civilian hurt.

His duty was to stay put.

So he would. For now. But this wasn't over. Not by a long shot.

TWO

Seeing Ryan faltering on his feet unsettled Meghan. He was usually so in control. She hurried back to his side. "You need to sit," she insisted and helped him to the curb next to Helen.

Tall, broad shouldered. Lean and muscled in his uniform, the man was ruggedly handsome with no hint of weakness behind the stony wall he put up every time she came near.

"This is unbelievable!" Ryan pounded one fist on his thigh.

Meghan drew away at the explosive wrath. Old fears spurted to life bringing back horrifying memories of her previous existence. Her ex-husband had had an explosive temper. And a mean streak as wide as the ocean. She had the scars to prove it. Her danger barometer rang a resounding alarm. The last thing she needed in her life was a man who couldn't control his anger.

Needing space, Meghan paced as she battled

to maintain her composure as well as her peace of mind.

She could feel Ryan's gaze like a touch as he traced her path. He was angry. Well, so was she. At the situation, at him. So much for her composure. She'd had Georgina in her grasp. Ryan was supposed to have protected them. She glared at him. "This shouldn't have happened."

He met her gaze, his icy-blue eyes dark with fury. "No, it shouldn't have." He shook his head, his face filled with self-loathing. "I let myself be distracted."

She frowned. "Distracted? By what?"

His gaze cut over her before he looked away. The muscle at the side of his jaw visibly pulsed. For a long moment she stared at his profile, at the angular lines of his cheekbones and straight nose, until something clicked in her mind. Did he mean he'd been distracted by her?

Her pulse tripped over itself. Her thoughts rewound to the moment inside the house when she'd been holding Georgina. Meghan had looked up to find Ryan in the doorway. She'd heard his voice long before he had appeared, so seeing him wasn't a surprise. But the look on his face…that had left her reeling.

She'd known from the get-go that this man was dangerous, on so many levels. It didn't help that every time she saw him she felt a flutter of feminine excitement.

Men in uniform could do that to a girl. And admittedly, Ryan filled out his blue uniform in a very eye-catching way that any woman with blood in her veins would notice.

But that didn't mean Meghan would repeat her past mistakes. She'd gone down the hunky-guy road before with disastrous results.

Not going there again. Especially not with a Fitzgerald. She didn't trust him. Couldn't even say she liked him.

Though admittedly, the wistful, almost yearning expression on Ryan's handsome face as he had watched her holding Georgina had both confused her and sent her pulse skittering.

Then he'd opened his mouth and all she'd registered at the time were the cold blue eyes and the hard set to his jaw that she'd grown used to seeing over the past six months in her campaign for more to be done in bringing her cousin's murderer to justice.

"Have you given any consideration to what could have happened had Christina and her thug returned before I got here?" Ryan asked, his blue gaze drilling through her.

She lifted a shoulder in a slight shrug. "But she didn't."

"Dumb luck."

Her gaze narrowed. "I don't believe in luck, Deputy Chief. I wouldn't have thought you did, either, considering you're a churchgoing man."

"My faith isn't the issue here. What concerns me is your lack of regard for your safety. For the safety of little Georgina."

His words drilled a hole through her anger. Guilt wormed its way to the surface. She probably had been too rash in coming here alone. "I should have called you," she conceded.

"You think?" he muttered. "If you hadn't been here, I would have been able to control the situation."

The censure in his tone dug at her, setting her defenses firing. "You don't know that. Christina Hennessy's crazy. You saw proof of that. You believe she killed her husband."

Saying the words aloud felt like stepping into rush-hour traffic. She and Ryan had no control; they didn't know when they'd be hit. Little Georgina's life hung in the balance at the hands of an unhinged gun-toting woman and a muscle-bound criminal with no aversion to pounding on people.

Christina Hennessy may not have only killed her husband, but Olivia, too.

Meghan had to keep pushing for justice. Olivia

deserved nothing less. And baby Georgina deserved to be protected, cared for.

She squeezed her eyes tight. Tears leaked from the corners. "Please, dear Lord, keep Georgina safe. Please let us find her."

When she opened her eyes, she found Ryan staring at her with an arrested look on his face.

Not one to usually pray aloud in public, the heat of a blush crept up her neck and into her cheeks. But she wouldn't apologize. She'd worked hard to reclaim her faith after having spent too many years feeling lost and abandoned by God.

"Why is Georgina so important to you?" Ryan asked. "It's more than just chasing a story about Burke's death. So what gives?"

The squall of sirens filled the air and an ambulance roared to a halt a few feet away, followed by a Revere police cruiser, saving her from answering.

She was chasing a story, that much was true. Working freelance meant pitching ideas to various news sources and hoping something stuck. The editor at the *Boston City News* had been enthused by the hooks she'd dangled: murder, small-town police corruption, a baby without a home.

But there was more, much more to this tale.

Georgina Hennessy was Olivia's biological child. And soon she'd have to tell Ryan that Olivia was his half sister. His father, Aiden Fitzgerald, had had an affair with Meghan's aunt Tara.

Not a conversation she was looking forward to, however necessary. She wasn't sure how the deputy chief would take the news.

Ryan struggled to stand. Meghan helped him, taking on some of his weight. The heat of his body engulfed her. He was still sweating from the fight. Being so close to him sent awareness skating over her. She forced herself to ignore the attractive draw of Deputy Chief Ryan Fitzgerald.

He was not her friend nor was he someone she could trust with her life or her heart.

Ryan winced as one of the paramedics wound tape about his midsection. The other paramedic probed at his ankle, setting Ryan's teeth on edge. He sat on the back bumper of an ambulance, having refused to be loaded on a gurney. He wasn't that hurt. He had work to do.

He still had to call in a report to the FB police station. Though he figured they'd probably already heard from the Revere Police Department about the injured Fitzgerald Bay officers. Ryan's gut churned.

Helen Yorke and Officer Jackson had already been transported to the hospital by the first ambulance to arrive. Both had probable concussions. By the time the paramedics had Jackson strapped to a gurney he'd regained consciousness. He needed stitches to his head and had a broken wrist. Apparently Christina had distracted Jackson while Jay snuck up behind him and clocked him good after a brief struggle.

Guilt for the rookie's injuries piled on top of the guilt Ryan already felt for allowing Christina and her henchman to escape with Georgina. His body hurt, but his injuries didn't ache nearly as bad as his heart.

It had to be the letdown of adrenaline from his brawl with the muscle-bound Jay and the helpless rage at having Christina take off with Georgina that had him all bound tight inside. Regardless, he couldn't keep his gaze from straying to where Meghan stood a few feet away, giving her statement to a female Revere patrol officer.

Meghan talked with her hands, expressing her mounting panic. So different than the soothing way she'd held little Georgina. The contrast fascinated Ryan. Now she seemed to be in constant motion. Under all that nervous energy hid a spine of steel. Thankfully she hadn't gone into hysterics during the scuffle with Christina and muscle boy. Meghan had done her best to protect the child.

Grudging respect for her crowded his chest.

He forced his gaze away from Meghan.

"Has Mrs. Hennessy been apprehended yet?"

Ryan called to the Revere officer who'd completed taking his statement a few moments ago.

Officer Garrett had been talking on his radio and now walked over. "The sedan was spotted going north on Highway 95."

Frustration knotted Ryan's stomach muscles. He wanted to go after them.

"Sir, you need to hold still," the young paramedic advised. "You've got at least two cracked ribs. And your ankle is badly sprained. You'll need X-rays. You could have a hairline fracture."

Great. A hobbled failure. "Just tape it up. I'll be fine."

Meghan finished giving her account of the events and walked quickly toward Ryan. His insides twisted at the dark bruise developing on her right cheek. Her face must hurt. "She could use some ice," he said to the second EMT.

The paramedic finished with his ribs, helped him with his T-shirt, then turned his attention to Meghan. Ryan gingerly shrugged back into his uniform shirt. His ribs hurt worse than when he'd come between his brother's baseball bat and his mom's front picture window.

Officer Garrett's radio crackled. He moved away to answer. Ryan could see from his expression that something was happening. He tried to stand, but the paramedic taping his ankle pressed him back down.

Officer Garrett approached. "They found the car and arrested the driver."

Ryan's nerves jumped. His jaw tightened. "Where?"

"Georgina?" Meghan asked, pushing past the paramedic who was tending to her bruised face to step closer, her wide eyes filled with hope and concern.

Officer Garrett shook his head. "Unfortunately, Mrs. Hennessy and the little girl were not with the man when the Portsmouth police picked him up."

Ryan tensed even more, sending pain shooting through his ribs. "How close was he to the Portsmouth International Airport?"

"A couple miles," Officer Garrett stated.

"At least they hadn't made it that far." Ryan hated the idea that Christina could have jetted off with Georgina before they could arrest her. "Still, have airport security keep a vigilant eye out."

The officer nodded and quickly relayed the message into his radio. Then he said, "The guy's not talking. He's being taken to the Portsmouth Police station."

The sound of heels clacking against pavement jerked Ryan's gaze around. Meghan was hurrying toward her Subaru.

He gripped his ribs and jumped up, keeping all his weight on his right leg. A spasm of pain washed over him. For a moment the world spun.

He pushed through the hurt and the dizziness. "Meghan, wait!"

"Sir, you shouldn't walk yet," admonished the EMT with concern in his voice.

Meghan ignored Ryan's cry and climbed inside her burgundy car.

Disregarding the paramedic's reprimand, Ryan hustled as fast as he could to the side of Meghan's small SUV, each step agony in his left foot. He rapped his knuckles on the driver's window. She turned the key in the ignition and powered down the window.

"You're not going to Portsmouth," Ryan said before the window was completely down. "You've meddled enough."

"You're not in charge of me," she snapped, her hazel eyes sparking with defiance. "Either you're coming with me or you're stepping back."

Ryan reached in and grabbed her wrist. "Do you want me to arrest you?"

When she tried to twist out of his grasp, he held firm.

"Get your hand off me," she said between clenched teeth.

"You are not going to Portsmouth."

"I don't believe you'd arrest me." Her sharp gaze sliced into him, but he was prepared to suffer whatever additional damage he had to endure to stop her. "You're going to sit here while my…

while that little girl is in danger? While Christina gets away? What kind of cop are you? That man they have in custody may know something useful. Something that will lead us to Christina and Georgina. Christina needs to be punished for her crimes. And that little girl needs to be protected."

Furious at her for questioning him and even madder that what she said was true, Ryan released his hold on her wrist and yanked on the door handle. Locked. "Unlock the door."

She shook her head, her blond hair sliding over her shoulder. "No. *You* get in."

Barely holding on to his temper, he forced himself to breathe. Arresting her would only be a temporary fix. The charges wouldn't hold. She'd be back out causing him problems before he could get new tires put on his vehicle.

Waiting for one of his brothers to come pick him up would take time. Time was not his friend here. Every second wasted meant Christina was getting farther away with Georgina. If the police didn't find her at the airport… The only person with any idea of where Christina and the child were going was the thug, Jay. Ryan needed to find out what he knew. Sooner rather than later.

"Scoot over. I'm driving," he ground out.

She scoffed. "Not on your life, buddy. You may need to be in control a hundred percent of the time, but this is my car, my rules. And I'm driving. Besides, in case you haven't noticed, you're hurt."

His fingers curled. A flash of fear crossed her face as quick as lightning, leaving Ryan momentarily disoriented. That was the second time he'd seen distress that had no basis. The woman was a paradox. Bold and brash, ready for a clash of wills at every moment, yet… He gave a dismissive shake of his head. Puzzling over her wasn't going to get Georgina back or put Christina behind bars.

"Fine." He hobbled around the front of the car, keeping his hand on the hood, forcing her to stay put or run him over. He wouldn't have been too surprised if she tried running him down.

He'd barely settled himself in the passenger seat when she hit the gas and barreled down the street. He slanted her a glance. She couldn't seem to keep still in her seat. Her shoulders were hiked up to her ears.

He pulled his cell phone from his pocket and called his brother Douglas.

"Where are you?" Douglas asked the moment he picked up. As the closest siblings in age, only thirteen months apart, Douglas and Ryan shared a bond of brotherhood and friendship as close as twins shared.

"Leaving Revere," Ryan answered. "We're headed to Portsmouth."

"Who's we?"

Ryan hesitated, then gave a mental shrug. Douglas would find out soon enough. "I'm with Meghan Henry."

"You took a civilian out in the field? What were you thinking?"

"I didn't take her anywhere," Ryan answered, his tone infused with the irritation coursing through his veins.

"We heard there were injuries."

"Jackson went to the hospital."

"And you?"

His rib pinched him, his ankle throbbed in time with his heartbeat. "Minor."

His brother snorted. "Nice try. Cracked ribs and a nasty sprained ankle aren't exactly minor."

Ryan tightened his grip on the phone. "I'm fine."

"Ryan?"

The concern in his brother's tone lanced through Ryan. "Hey, look, this is the deal. I'm following a lead on Christina Hennessy. I'll call again when I have something worth sharing."

"Let me get this straight. You're following a lead with Meghan Henry, a civilian, a reporter, while you're injured." Douglas paused. "Dude, the woman is Olivia Henry's cousin. She's totally biased and emotionally involved."

"You don't think I know this?" Ryan shifted away from Meghan and dropped his voice. "Better to keep her close so I can control the situation."

"Does Dad know?"

"He knows I'm following a lead on Christina Hennessy." As chief of police, Aiden Fitzgerald kept a firm and fair grip on the department. Just as Ryan would do when he took over as chief after his father won the upcoming mayoral election.

"Be careful, brother."

His gaze shot to Meghan. He'd allowed himself to be distracted by her once. There wouldn't be a repeat. "I plan to."

He hung up. Then made the necessary calls to Portsmouth, alerting them he was coming. When he finished his calls, he turned to Meghan. "They'll contact me if there are any new developments."

Leaning back into the seat, his aches clamored for dominance in his consciousness. He tried taking a decent breath. Sharp pain was his reward. A glance at the dashboard clock told him they were making good time. Meghan had a lead foot. If he wasn't so anxious to get to Portsmouth, he'd point out she was pushing the speed limit.

Her nails drummed on the steering wheel as she maneuvered the Subaru through traffic. Pink nail polish on neatly filed fingernails. Long, tapered fingers.

He could imagine Meghan running her fingers through his hair, over his shoulders....

Needing to keep his mind from rabbiting down

a hole that he had no business exploring, he redirected his thoughts to the situation. "What sent you to Helen Yorke's house?"

"I heard that the charm found near Olivia's body belonged to Christina Hennessy. When I went to the Hennessys' house, Christina and Georgina were gone. I figured her ex-housekeeper might have an idea where Christina would disappear to. They'd seemed close before Helen left town."

A cold finger of dread ran down his back. "Who told you about the charm?"

A leaky police department drowned a lot of good people over time. That information was supposed to be quiet until they could bring Christina in. They'd only recently released the image of the silver dolphin charm that had been discovered at the crime scene of Olivia Henry's murder. A reliable tip had pointed them in Christina's direction. Topping that off with the evidence linking Christina to Burke's death…

"Sorry. A good reporter never reveals a source."

Irritation flared. His jaw tightened. "Well, you found her didn't you?"

Meghan remained silent, letting the sarcasm of his words fill the car. "The paper said Burke died of a heart attack, but I'd heard it was a prescription overdose. Some say on purpose." She glanced at him.

He didn't think keeping the information from

her would serve much purpose. It would become public knowledge soon enough. "No. No heart attack, no overdose, at least not on purpose. Asphyxiation was the official cause of death."

Ryan had never bought the theory that Burke offed himself. The socially ambitious lawyer had been too set on usurping any Fitzgerald claim to the mayor's seat to be suicidal. He'd been one of two men who thought Fitzgerald Bay needed new blood in the town government. "There's evidence of foul play. Fibers found in his nostrils and throat suggested he'd also been smothered with a pillow, finishing off what the drugs had started."

"That's horrible."

Ryan ran a hand through his hair. "You never answered my question. Why is Georgina so important to you?"

She pressed her lips tightly together, the corners pinching slightly. After a moment, she said, "I received a letter earlier today."

"And that has to do with Georgina how?"

Looking suddenly uncertain, she hesitated. Seeming to debate with herself, she nodded once, straightened her shoulders and briefly met his gaze. "It was from Olivia, postmarked before her death."

He drew back in surprise. "You just now got it?"

A flash of impatience sparked in her hazel eyes as she slanted him a sharp glance. "Yes. When I left Boston, I didn't have a forwarding address, so the super of my building held my mail. He finally got around to sending it all to me."

"Do you have the letter with you?"

"No. It's in a safe place." She inhaled and then released a breath before saying, "How did you find out Olivia had a child?"

"I should be asking you that question." But he figured she wouldn't tell him anyway. That leak needed to be plugged. "The autopsy revealed she'd given birth." Confirming what they'd already suspected. He hesitated a moment, then decided to tell her what else they'd discovered, though she probably already knew. Why did he feel like he was being tested? "A box, postmarked from Fitzgerald Bay, arrived at the police station."

Perking up with curiosity, she prompted, "What was in it?"

"A pink baby blanket, a baby bracelet from a hospital in Ireland with the words *Henry Baby Girl* and the name of a doctor and a date, and an uncashed check for ten thousand dollars made out to Olivia Henry. None of which has helped to find Olivia's killer or identify the person who mailed the box."

She glanced at him. "But surely the doctor or the hospital had some useful information on what happened to the baby."

"The hospital had a break-in not long after

Olivia gave birth. Her records are missing. The doctor didn't have any useful information other than confirming she'd delivered Olivia's baby girl."

Seeming to weigh his words, she adjusted her grip on the steering wheel. "Why didn't you tell me this sooner?"

"It was privileged information in an ongoing investigation," he stated.

She made a little frustrated noise low in her throat. "Apparently Olivia had given her child up for adoption. But then regretted her decision and wanted her baby back."

"Is that what she wrote in her letter?"

"Yes."

Empathy twisted in his chest. "Unfortunately, there's no way to confirm that supposition."

She adjusted her grip on the wheel. "Yes, there is. The adoption was illegal and Olivia had been tricked into signing away her rights. Olivia tracked down her baby girl and found her in Fitzgerald Bay. That was why she'd moved from Ireland to the U.S. She wanted her baby back. Olivia wanted her baby girl to be with me if anything happened to her. She apparently didn't feel safe in Fitzgerald Bay."

Something niggled at the back of Ryan's brain. "And she knew who had adopted her child?"

Meghan nodded. "Christina and Burke Hennessy."

He stilled. "Georgina is Olivia's child?"

He pictured the little girl with her blond curls and bright blue eyes safe in Meghan's arms. No wonder Meghan had held the child so tenderly with so much love. She believed the toddler to be her cousin's daughter.

He remembered when the Hennessys brought the baby home, claiming they'd adopted her, thus rescuing her from a drug addict in New York City. The Hennessys must have known the adoption was illegal and could be challenged if they were tracked down as the adoptive parents by the birth mother. No one had questioned them. There hadn't been any reason to.

"Maybe Olivia confronted Christina and Christina killed Olivia to keep Georgina," Meghan reasoned.

"It's a good theory. There's evidence that could link her to the crime." If so, he had the motive they'd been searching for in Olivia's murder. "But why would Christina kill Burke if they were in this together?"

"I don't know. Maybe he found out Christina killed Olivia and threatened to turn her in or said they'd have to come clean about the illegal adoption, give the baby to the authorities."

"Maybe," he said. What a complicated mess.

"You believe me, then?" Meghan asked, her voice tense. "Or rather, Olivia?"

This woman was related to the deceased and

to the baby that may have been the catalyst for Olivia's murder. "I don't know why you'd lie."

"I wouldn't. I don't lie."

He could only take her word on that.

Meghan flipped on her blinker and took the exit ramp for Portsmouth. "Do you know how to get to the police station?"

He arched an eyebrow. "Do you always start driving without knowing where you're going?"

Her mouth tightened. "I figured I'd ask for directions when I arrived. But since you're with me, I'd hoped you'd know where to go."

Shaking his head, he searched for the address on his smartphone and directed her. A few minutes later they pulled up to the square redbrick building of the Portsmouth police headquarters.

Large green, manicured hedges framed the walkway. Summer sun reflected off the paved sidewalk in hot waves, but a slight breeze coming off the Atlantic Ocean a few miles away kept the heat bearable.

Ryan hobbled to the glass front door in Meghan's wake. She held open the door for him then herded him to the desk sergeant.

Ryan glared at her. He wasn't limping that badly. He identified himself to the sergeant.

A moment later, a man wearing the navy uniform of the Portsmouth Police Department approached.

The stars on the collar of his uniform alerted Ryan to the man's rank even before he spoke.

"Deputy Chief Fitzgerald, I've been expecting you." They shook hands. "I'm Chief Danhoff. We've got the suspect in a room. We've read him his rights and he's declined a lawyer. I was waiting for you before questioning him."

Chief Danhoff assessed Meghan. "And you are?"

"This is Meghan Henry. She's a blood relative of the missing child."

"Ah. You'll want to observe then." Motioning for them to follow, Chief Danhoff led the way. He opened a door. "Miss Henry you can watch from in here."

Meghan disappeared inside.

Ryan followed Danhoff into the interrogation room. He was determined to bring down Christina Hennessy and find the little girl.

THREE

Meghan took a deep breath and slowly exhaled. Nope, didn't calm her nerves any. Gathering her courage like a shield, she stepped inside the Portsmouth observation room and watched Ryan enter the interrogation room. The small space seemed even more cramped with the big, muscle-bound Jay sitting at a metal table. She couldn't see his hands. She assumed they were handcuffed to his chair or something.

Surprise flickered in Jay's dark eyes when he saw Ryan. "What are you doing here?"

"I need answers and you're going to give them to me," Ryan said, bracing his hands on the table and leaning into Jay's face.

"Fat chance, pretty boy," Jay spat out, testing the strength of the cuffs holding his arms at his sides.

"Did you help Christina Hennessy kill her husband?"

Jay drew back. "I don't know nothing about no husband and no death. Wasn't me."

"Mrs. Hennessy didn't tell you about murdering her husband?"

Jay frowned. "Naw. She just needed some brawn for the day."

A muscle ticked in Ryan's jaw. "What rock did she find you under?"

When Jay didn't respond, Ryan slapped a hand on the table, the crack echoed off the walls. Meghan felt the impact through the glass. Her heart jolted.

"You're going down, Jay. Assault on a police officer, kidnapping—"

"I didn't kidnap anyone!" Jay protested.

"And you'll be charged as an accomplice in Burke Hennessy's murder."

"I'm telling you I don't know this Burke guy, and I didn't kill anyone."

"Then tell me how you hooked up with Christina," Ryan said, his tone intense.

With a sullen pout, Jay said, "She came into the Last Stand bar asking if anyone wanted to make a quick grand."

"When was this?"

Jay shrugged. "Just this morning."

"She gave you a thousand dollars to do what?"

"Oh, I got more than a measly thou," Jay said, pride puffing up his chest. "Since I was the only one in the bar, she didn't have much choice. I wanted five grand."

Surprise washed over Meghan.

"She had that much cash on her?" Ryan voiced the question rising inside Meghan.

"Yeah. I could tell she was rich. Liked to look down her nose at others. I know the type."

Christina had obviously been planning her escape to have so much cash at the ready.

"What did she want you to do?"

He shrugged. "To go with her to get the kid and make sure they got to the airport safely."

"Do you know where they were planning to fly to?"

He shook his head. "Naw. She thought I was just a big dumb guy she could boss around. For five grand, I let her."

"Which airline did you drop her off at?"

Jay shook his head. "Didn't. She changed her mind."

Ryan pinned him with a look. "Then where is Christina and the toddler now?"

He shrugged. "Don't know."

Meghan pressed her hands against the glass willing the man to talk.

"Where did you leave them?" Ryan's tone echoed with irritation.

"She wanted to be dropped off at the mall."

Meghan's stomach sank.

"Mall? Where? Which one?" Ryan asked

sharply. His gaze strayed to the mirrored wall and bounced away.

"The fancy one, near the expressway."

"Did she talk to anyone?" Ryan pressed. "Was she meeting someone there?"

Jay shook his head. "I didn't see anyone. But she could have been meeting someone. She made a call on her cell."

Meghan's pulse sped up. She strained forward. "Did you hear a name?"

"Naw. She was talking real low. Couldn't hear anything. She sat in the back like I was her chauffeur or something."

"You didn't hear anything to let you know where she was headed or what her plans were?" Doubt infused Ryan's tone.

"Naw, man. That's all I know."

Ryan straightened and nodded to the chief who'd hung back without saying a word. The men exited the room.

Meghan met Ryan in the hall. Chief Danhoff headed away. "We have to get back to Revere. To the Northgate Shopping Center, it's right off the Northeast Expressway."

"Chief's already making contact with Revere P.D."

"Let's go!" She turned toward the door.

Ryan snagged her elbow and held on. "We're

going to let the Revere P.D. handle this. You've done enough."

She jerked her arm out of his grasp. "You can stay here. But I'm going to the mall."

His frustrated growl sent a shiver down her back as she rushed for the front door.

"Hold up." Ryan's agitated voice halted her as she pushed open the glass doors. He limped as fast as he could toward her, each step bringing a wince of pain. Empathy rose. She knew what it was like to have to function while hurt. The abuse she'd suffered at the hands of her ex-husband had made some days nearly unbearable.

He reached her side. "Can we at least wait to see if the mall security can locate them? We don't know whether or not she had another car already waiting to whisk them away."

"But we have to do something!"

"You're right. But us driving all over the place chasing our tails is not going to bring Georgina back. We need to be patient."

"Easy for you to say," she muttered.

He looked her in the eye. "No, actually, it's not."

She believed him. He was a man of action, used to being in control. He was a Fitzgerald, after all. He was probably accustomed to snapping his fingers and having the world jump to attention. Even as the uncharitable thought formed she dismissed it. Ryan may be many things but pompous wasn't one of them.

Chief Danhoff halted beside Ryan. "Mall security has locked down the mall and the Revere P.D. is on the scene. We'll know something shortly."

"Good." Ryan looked at Meghan expectantly.

Conflicted, she hesitated. She wanted to jump in the car and hightail it back to Revere, but if Christina and Georgina weren't at the mall, then the trip would be wasted. Better to stay put and be ready to move when they were found. She acquiesced and released her hold on the door.

The seconds ticked by. Meghan tapped one foot in a rhythmic cadence. Ryan placed a hand on her arm. The light contact stilled her nerves in a way she'd never experienced before. The tapping stopped. It wasn't an unpleasant sensation, yet it left her feeling vulnerable. She frowned and moved away from his touch. Instantly her nerves jumped to life. She paced the length of the entryway.

"Chief," called the desk sergeant, holding up a phone. "It's the Revere P.D."

Anticipation grabbed hold of Meghan as she and Ryan followed Danhoff toward the phone. Danhoff took the call, listened for a moment then thanked the officer on the other end. His grim expression turned Meghan's blood cold.

"The Revere police did a thorough search. Mrs. Hennessy and her daughter are nowhere to be found."

Meghan fought back tears. She'd had Georgina in her arms. Anxiety fisted in her chest, creating a deep ache that nearly drove her to her knees. Her last remaining relative was in danger.

"What about security cameras?" Ryan asked.

Danhoff shook his head. "They have them entering through the south entrance of the mall and going inside one of the big department stores. They lost them in the women's restroom. They never came out."

"How can that be?" Meghan questioned, her voice rising with disbelief. "Someone had to have seen them."

"Christina was prepared. She most likely had a disguise ready and changed her and Georgina's appearance in the bathroom." Ryan ran a hand through his short-cropped dark hair. "I can't believe this."

Meghan couldn't, either. The trail had gone ice cold. Despair and fear clawed at her throat. Tears stung her eyes.

Now what?

Traffic on the way back to Fitzgerald Bay added to Meghan's frustration. Not only had they lost

Georgina, they had no idea where to look for her. Christina could have taken her anywhere.

Heart aching, Meghan sent up a silent prayer of protection for Georgina.

In the passenger seat Ryan shifted, again. From the moment they'd left the Portsmouth Police Department, he'd been restless and kept looking in the side-view mirror.

"What are you doing?" she finally asked after he turned in his seat with a groan, because of his hurt ribs, to stare out the back window for the umpteenth time.

"We have a tail," he stated, facing forward again.

She frowned. "A tail? Like in being followed?"

"Yeah, exactly like."

She glanced through the rearview mirror at the multitude of cars dotting the highway behind them. "There's so much traffic. How can you tell?"

"There's a silver van about five cars back. I saw it at the police station. It's been keeping the same distance for the past ten miles."

"Coincidence?"

"Maybe. Maybe not." He gestured ahead. "Take the next exit."

She signaled and moved over to the far-right lane. In the rearview mirror she noticed the van did the same. Her heart pounded in her chest as she took the exit ramp. The van sped up and barreled down the ramp behind them.

"Ryan?" The light at the end of the ramp turned red. She pressed on the brakes, the car skidding to a halt. The van pulled up alongside the car. The back panel door slid open. Masked men aimed big black guns at them.

"Get down!" Ryan yelled.

Meghan screamed and ducked as a spray of gunfire pelted the car. The side window shattered. She felt a stinging sensation in her shoulder.

Reflexively, she stomped on the gas to get away from the flying bullets. The Subaru jolted forward through the red light. Horns blared. Tires squealed on pavement as cars swerved to avoid hitting them. She yanked on the steering wheel to prevent them from ramming into a streetlight. The back window exploded into a million pieces.

"Keep driving!" Ryan shouted.

She didn't have to be told twice. She kept her foot pressed on the gas and swerved around a car.

This couldn't be happening.

The whole event seemed surreal, like she'd stepped into some action movie by mistake.

She turned down a side street and another and another until she had no sense of where they were or what direction they were headed. The van wasn't following them now, but that didn't lessen her panic. Her shoulder throbbed, her arm and hand numb. Ryan spoke to her. His phone in his hand, she could see his lips moving when she glanced his way, but only heard the rush of adrenaline in her ears.

He placed a hand over hers on the steering wheel. His touch grounded her. Through a foggy haze she heard his voice.

"Meghan, come on, Meghan, I need you to hold it together. Slow the car down."

She eased her foot from the gas. The car's acceleration dropped.

"Put your foot on the brake," Ryan instructed.

She did as asked. Allowing him to guide her hands, she pulled the car to the curb, halting at an odd angle. Smoke curled from under the Subaru's hood. She began to shake.

"You're bleeding!" Ryan quickly undid his seat belt and bolted from the car.

He limped around to her side of the car and yanked open the driver's door. Carefully, he eased her out of the seat. The world swam and she clung to him for support. He helped her to sit on the curb.

Her dress was covered in brown sticky stuff. She frowned. Her left hand was covered in it, too.

Blood.

The thought slammed into her mind, sending waves of shock through her system. She was bleeding. Nausea churned, she clamped her mouth tight. She would not throw up on him.

Ryan took off his blue uniform shirt and then

his white T-shirt, revealing the nasty bruises peeking out from under the bandage wrapped around his torso. He bunched the T-shirt into a ball and pressed it to her shoulder. Pain zinged at the point of contact.

Her mind grappled to make sense of why he was doing that.

Reality crashed in. She'd been shot. She swayed.

"Put your head between your knees," Ryan said, pushing her head down with gentle pressure.

After a moment the world stopped spinning. The sounds of sirens sent a tremor coursing over her flesh. Twice in one day they were waiting for an ambulance.

Thank You, Lord, for Your protection.

"Who were those men?" she asked Ryan when she felt steady enough to raise her head.

His mouth pressed into a grim line. "I don't know."

"Do you think this is connected to Christina?"

"Could be. Maybe. I don't know."

"Are you working on another case? Someone who wants you dead?" she asked, reaching for some explanation.

"No." He peered at her. "What about you? What are you working on?"

"Just my cousin's murder."

At the reminder, she shuddered. Her cousin had been murdered, and now someone had tried to kill her and Ryan. Was this attempt on their lives connected in some way to Olivia's death? Had Christina orchestrated the masked gunmen?

"Is the dolphin charm the only evidence you have that Christina might be involved in Olivia's murder?" she asked, hoping to piece the facts together.

"There was a second blood sample found on the rock used to kill Olivia. DNA testing finally eliminated my brother Charles as a suspect. I wouldn't be surprised if Christina Hennessy's DNA is all over that rock."

She was glad his brother was no longer a suspect in Olivia's death. Charles Fitzgerald had been Olivia's employer. She'd been his twins' nanny. Meghan knew Olivia had loved those kids.

"When the charm was identified as Christina's," he continued, "I wondered. Then she skipped town with Georgina, coupled with Burke's death…leads me to believe she's got a dark side. Now we know for sure she's capable of violence. When we take Christina into custody, we'll run her DNA. If it matches…"

"Then she was at least there when Olivia was killed. She could have been struck with the same rock, for all you know."

"True. Unless she confesses, the evidence places her at the crime scene but doesn't make her a murderer."

Meghan's reporter instincts were clamoring,

sensing a bigger story than she'd originally anticipated. One worthy of catapulting her career forward. Just what the story entailed she had yet to
determine. "But Ryan, if these masked gunmen
are connected to Christina, then whatever she's
into, it's bigger than my cousin's or Burke Hennessy's death."

He ran a hand through his hair. "You're right.
But I don't have a clue what she's gotten herself
into or how big it is."

Setting aside the lure of a big story for the moment, she put her hand on his. "Promise me, Ryan,
the priority will be getting Georgina back safely."

He covered her hand with his. "I promise."

She swallowed a tide of unease. She could only
hope once she told him the truth about Olivia's
parentage he'd be a man of his word and keep his
promise.

The next morning, Ryan sat at his desk staring out the window of his office in the fishing
village where he'd grown up. It was a beautiful
June day, the sun was shining, a nice breeze blew
in from the bay, and the townspeople were busy
with their lives despite that fact that twice in the
past six months there'd been a murder in their
quiet haven. Two more than there'd been in the
past several decades.

Frustration beat a steady tempo behind his eyes.

The town and its people wouldn't be safe until he got to the bottom of Olivia Henry's and Burke Hennessy's deaths.

But did those two murders have anything to do with the van that ambushed him and Meghan yesterday?

The van was nowhere to be found, Christina Hennessy and little Georgina were still missing, and Ryan's father wanted to call in the FBI. Ryan knew they should. Their police department wasn't equipped to do a full-scale investigation across state lines. But losing the case chafed.

A knock at his door brought up his gaze. Meghan Henry stood in the doorway. His breath caught in his chest. Her cheek still bore the mark from the hit she'd taken by Christina's thug. But nothing could detract from the natural beauty she exuded. Today she wore white capris and a light purple flowing top. She looked like a fairy princess. All she needed was a crown of flowers.

He frowned. When did he become so whimsical? That wasn't like him. "Morning, Meghan. How's your shoulder?"

She briefly touched the place on her shoulder where a bullet had grazed her. The bandage covering the wound wasn't visible beneath her top. "Doctor says it will hurt for a while, but will heal." Dropping her hand, she asked, "How are your injuries?"

"Barely noticeable." Except when he breathed real deep. But admitting to the vulnerability wasn't going to happen.

She strode forward and stopped at the edge of his desk in a swirl of energy. "Has there been any news about Georgina?"

"No, I'm sorry, there hasn't been. I'm about to call the FBI and hand over the case to them."

She drew back. "No. You promised you'd find Georgina."

"Meghan, this is bigger than this department can handle. Christina has crossed state lines. Though technically, she hasn't kidnapped her child."

Anger flashed in her hazel eyes. "But Georgina's not hers!"

He understood her upset but he had to follow the law. "That's for a judge to decide."

"Georgina's in danger. You saw Christina. She's nuts. If nothing else, she held a cop at gunpoint. Surely that warrants you pursuing her."

"We're doing everything in our power to bring her in."

"You maybe, but not your father. He's as responsible for Olivia's death as Christina."

"My father?" The woman had obviously lost her mind. Maybe the blow to the head had loosened something. "What are you talking about?"

She waved a letter in the air. The letter from Olivia, he guessed.

"Your father knew that Olivia had come to Fitzgerald Bay looking for her baby girl, and he chose to ignore her pleas for help."

He let out a scoff full of annoyance. "That is untrue. My father barely knew Olivia."

"Really? Is that what he told you?" She shook her head. "I'm not going to let you all sweep this under the rug. If your father had done the right thing to begin with Olivia would never… Her life would have been different. Better. She wouldn't be dead now."

Fury swept over him at the implication in her words. "What are you saying?"

"Your father is also Olivia's biological father. Olivia's your half sister."

No! Not possible. His father was the best man he knew, as solid a citizen as they came. A church-going man who loved the Lord. The role model Ryan could only hope to live up to. Dad would not have ever cheated on his wife. They'd had the best marriage, until Maureen Fitzgerald had passed away from cancer a few years ago. Her death had hit them all hard.

Now this reporter was disparaging his father. He'd see Meghan Henry locked behind bars before he'd let her destroy his family.

FOUR

Meghan waited, watching Ryan as he absorbed her announcement. The blue shirt of his uniform matched his eyes. Eyes that now gathered storm clouds. She'd known this wouldn't be easy, and he wouldn't take it well. But the truth had to come out.

Her body tensed, ready to react if he so much as twitched in her direction.

He remained very, very still. "How dare you make such a slanderous claim."

"I'm not claiming it. *Olivia* is." She'd been as shocked as he apparently was when she'd read the letter that outlined how Olivia had sought help with the situation from her biological father when she first arrived in Fitzgerald Bay. Aiden Fitzgerald had refused. "Your father and my aunt Tara had an affair."

In one fluid, swift motion, he reached across his desk and snatched the letter from her hands before she even had time to react.

Stunned, her heart hammered in her chest and blood pounded at her temples. So much for those self-defense classes she'd taken. They hadn't prepared her for Ryan Fitzgerald's ninjalike moves.

Ryan unfolded Olivia's letter and read the contents. His face paled. He shook his head. "This can't be true."

"You believed her about Georgina," she pointed out.

She'd known the news wouldn't be received well. She'd witnessed how the breath of scandal had rocked the Fitzgerald clan over the past few months as Charles Fitzgerald had become the number one suspect in Olivia's murder.

Now with him cleared, she was sure the family would do all they could to keep this information about Olivia's parentage from surfacing. But she couldn't allow that. Aiden Fitzgerald had helped take away Meghan's one known remaining relative. Meghan would make sure he atoned for his part in Olivia's death, because now her only living relation was missing and in danger.

"My father wouldn't have done such a thing." Ryan's voice shook with rage and disbelief. "And if you breathe a word of this to the public, I'll lock you up so fast you won't know what hit you."

Oh, she'd known all right. But she was done being anyone's victim, even a gorgeous lawman's.

She'd ditched that label a long time ago. Meghan would only bow down for God.

"You can't suppress the truth," she said. "You read the letter. Olivia came here and contacted her father first. He refused to help her. If he had done what he should have, she wouldn't be dead now."

"There's no proof of any of this." He reached into a desk drawer and pulled out a thick file. He flipped through until he found what he was looking for. Holding up a sheet of paper, he said, "This is Olivia's birth certificate from Ireland. There is no name listed under *father*."

"That's because your father refused to acknowledge her. It was heartbreaking to read Olivia's words of the father who hadn't wanted her, but she had known about him her whole life. That's why she came to him for help."

"I refuse to believe it." The letter fluttered to the desktop.

"Doesn't matter if you want to or not, it's the truth." She reached for the letter.

He grasped her wrist with firm, but gentle pressure. The fight-or-flight response roared through her system like a runaway train engine. She reacted instantaneously, calling upon the self-defense classes she'd taken last year, by twisting her arm and jerking toward where his thumb lay against her wrist bone, knowing that was the weak point of his hold. She broke the contact and jumped back. She'd come a long way from the frightened young woman who'd been too afraid to do anything but accept the way her husband treated her.

They stared at each other for a long, tense moment. Ryan's cold blue eyes drilled through her. She regained her step, aware on some level she had messed with his control. She rather liked having some leverage.

"I think you should leave." He rounded the desk and crowded her back several steps.

The urge to cower gripped her, but she held her ground. However she couldn't stop the instinctive flinch as he reached past her to open the door. His big warm body didn't touch her, but the air swirled around her with his heat. The spicy scent of his aftershave filled her head, invading her senses. Her fingers curled into fists. She didn't want him inside her head.

"Run along now, Miss Henry," he said, stepping back.

Being dismissed like some errant child infuriated her to no end. "Look, you don't have to like me, but you have to treat me with respect."

"Respect?" He nearly sneered. "You come into my office and accuse my father of..." He made a noise in his throat. "You could have written that letter, for all I know."

"I didn't!"

He leaned in close, his voice tight and low. "Are you working for Judge Monroe? Has he put you up to this? Trying to smear my father now that the judge's chances of winning the election are as good as gone because everyone knows he raised a bad seed?"

"Of course not," she protested, strangely hurt by the suspicion written all over his face. She'd been as horrified as the rest of the folks in town to learn that the judge's son, Hank Monroe, one of Fitzgerald Bay's police officers, had tried to hurt Victoria Evans, the owner of the Sugar Plum Café and Inn.

If not for Ryan's brother Owen, Victoria and her daughter would have been seriously injured, if not killed. And now Owen and Victoria were a couple. Again. Apparently, they'd been in love long ago but then Victoria had left town and only recently returned. With the daughter Owen didn't know about. Seemed the Fitzgerald clan were chock-full of drama and intrigue.

A good thing for Meghan and the story she was piecing together about Olivia's life and murder. And the investigation by the Fitzgerald Bay Police Department.

Ryan narrowed his gaze. "What are you after, Miss Henry?"

"The truth. Justice. And I want to make sure Georgina is found safely."

For a moment he studied her, his gaze bold and assessing. She returned the favor. There was an intrinsic strength in the angles of his face, the slope of his nose, the firmness of his lips. She had the sudden craving to lay her palm against his clean-shaven jaw to see if the skin was really as smooth as it appeared. His features struck a fine balance between rugged and handsome.

A flutter whipped through her and she deliberately squashed the wayward attraction knocking at her consciousness.

He drew in a deep breath and slowly let it out. "Then we want the same things."

"Okay, good." At least they were on the same page.

Though she had a feeling this wasn't going to end well for one of them. She wanted justice for her cousin, safety for Georgina, and her job as a reporter was to expose the truth, regardless that doing so would tarnish the reputation of Aiden Fitzgerald.

A truth Ryan would just as soon suppress. He wanted justice because of his duty to serve and protect, but not at the cost of his family. Too bad.

Deciding it was time to retreat, she turned to storm away, but found her nose buried in a man's chest. With a squawk she jerked back, bumping against Ryan's hard chest. With Ryan behind her and his imposing father filling the doorway, she was sandwiched between Fitzgeralds.

Police Chief Aiden Fitzgerald regarded her with the famous Fitzgerald baby blues. Only his eyes didn't hold the same sort of coldness that his eldest son's did. Not nearly as tall as his son, he was still very attractive with salt-and-pepper hair that was beginning to recede. "What's the matter here? I heard raised voices."

"Miss Henry was just leaving."

Oh, he'd like it if she meekly scuttled off like some bug he'd rather squish than deal with. Well, he had another thing coming. "As a matter of fact, Chief Fitzgerald, I was hoping to speak to you."

She ducked around Ryan and retreated back to the belly of his office, forcing both men to follow. Taking advantage of the fact that Ryan was too far away to try his lightning-fast ninja moves on her, she picked up the letter and turned to face the two Fitzgerald men.

A gale force of rage swept across Ryan's face. She swallowed hard, but refused to be intimidated by his clear displeasure. She addressed the elder Fitzgerald. "This is a letter from my cousin, Olivia."

She held out the sheet of paper. "You should read this."

Aiden took the letter. As he silently read the words written by his daughter, Meghan shifted her gaze to Ryan. His expression had turned to stone, his hands clenched at his sides, his back ramrod straight.

He stared out the large window behind his desk, but she doubted he saw the crystal-blue June sky or the quaint New England fishing village named after his family. Even standing completely motionless, vitality radiated off him like some invisible force field that drew her in instead of repelling her.

It didn't make sense. She shouldn't find this man attractive. Well, okay, the outward package was appealing; there was no denying that. Tall, broad shouldered, lean and a face that could grace a magazine cover were all well and good in an abstract sort of way.

But she shouldn't be noticing or caring. The last thing she wanted in her life was an overbearing, control freak. Once in a lifetime was enough, thank you very little.

Though she couldn't erase the memory of the kind and compassionate way he'd treated her yesterday when they'd been shot at. When she'd been shot. Her shoulder ached something fierce, but the pain medication the doctor gave her kept the throbbing to a dull roar.

Ryan's gaze slid to meet hers. She'd been staring and he'd caught her. One dark eyebrow rose ever so slightly. A blush worked its way up her neck but she would not look away. She wouldn't give him the satisfaction of backing down. Not that she believed Ryan's ego would be fed by her shrinking like a wilted flower. He wasn't like her ex-husband who enjoyed seeing her cower.

Aiden cleared his throat; there was a sickly pallor about his complexion. His pensive expression was unexpected. Meghan tensed. Where were the vehement denials she'd anticipated? He sat in Ryan's chair and held his head in his hands.

"Dad?" Ryan's voice held a note of uncertainty.

"We need an emergency family meeting at the house. I want everyone there at nine o'clock, tomorrow morning." Aiden strode to the door, the letter clutched in his hand. He paused and glanced back. "Ryan, bring Miss Henry with you."

Ryan stared after his father in confusion. Had he lost his mind? Bring Meghan to the house?

Ryan recoiled at the idea. Bringing anyone to the house meant one of two things: significant other or old and trusted friend. Meghan certainly wasn't either, and Ryan had never brought anyone home. *Serious* and *relationship* didn't belong together in his vocabulary.

But the more pressing question was why hadn't his dad set the record straight and told Meghan the letter was a fake?

Because it was true?

The thought streaked through his brain setting him back a step.

No! It couldn't be true. He refused to believe it. His father wouldn't have cheated on his mother. Never!

His father had to be calling a family meeting to refute Olivia's claim and prepare the family for another unsubstantiated scandal.

As if the family hadn't suffered enough these past six months with all the speculation and conjecture about Charles having murdered Olivia.

Add in his father's bid for mayor against a judge and a lawyer, both of whom reveled in every bit of dirt they could dig up on the family, and it had been a rough few months. His head pounded. Thinking of all they'd endured exhausted him. Imagining there could be more with this letter...

"Will you pick me up? Or should I meet you there?" Meghan asked, impatience lacing her words.

Drawing himself up, he marshaled his control and strode out of the office. The pesky woman grated across his nerves like an out-of-tune guitar. "You can meet me here at 8:45."

The next morning Meghan arrived at the police station a few minutes early in a rental car. She didn't want to give Ryan any excuses for leaving without her—though she could have easily found the Fitzgerald home on her own.

The place was quiet on this early Wednesday morning. She found Ryan in his office, sitting with his back to the door. She knocked. He straightened and slowly turned. He looked tired and haunted. Dark circles ringed his blue eyes.

"I'm ready," she said as nerves tumbled through her.

He rose, his wide shoulders blocking out part of the sun streaming through the window behind him. With long purposeful strides, he crossed the room and squeezed past her through the door. "Come along, Miss Henry."

Meghan made a face at Ryan's retreating back. It was all she could do not to stick her tongue out at him. She wasn't his lackey. If anything, he was hers. He might have a handsome face and shoulders wide enough to carry his entire family, but she wouldn't let that affect her. The sooner she established herself as an equal the better.

She hurried outside to catch up to him. An ocean-scented breeze whipped at her loose hair. The briny air reminded her of lazy summer days when she was a kid and her parents would take her to the seaside at Martha's Vineyard. Those carefree days were long gone.

Pushing back the stray strands with one hand,

she gestured to the blue sedan parked in the visitor's parking lot with her other hand. "I'll follow you."

He didn't respond as he climbed into his police-issue vehicle. Not that she expected him to. He was a regular caveman. At least today. But she knew there was hero material lurking somewhere in his cold heart.

He started the engine. Obviously, he'd had the tires replaced. She hurried to her car so she wouldn't be left in the dust.

How would the family react to having an outsider in their midst? Especially once they learned the truth? She shored up her courage. She'd faced worse, scarier situations in her life. A roomful of Fitzgeralds wouldn't daunt her determination. Besides, seeing their reactions would add depth to the article she planned to write. An article that should propel her career forward and bring justice to her cousin.

Less than ten minutes later, Meghan parked her car behind Ryan's in front of the colonial-style house that sat up on a gentle rise overlooking the town and the expansive Atlantic Ocean. The house sat on the highest ground above the village. All the wealthier citizens of Fitzgerald Bay had houses on the hill. The Hennessy home was a few doors down. A regular who's who of Fitzgerald Bay.

Meghan appreciated the clean look of the white home with its symmetrical windows flanking the white pillars on the front porch, giving the place a grand air. Sunlight gleamed off the leaded, decorative glass in the massive front door.

Flowers bloomed from window boxes attached beneath the five windows marching across the second floor. She'd only seen the house from a distance and had admired it.

Now here she was entering into the Fitzgerald inner sanctum. Something she had never expected. Yet couldn't deny she'd watched the family and yearned to belong to the tight-knit clan. If only she were visiting under more pleasant circumstances. A part of her wished she didn't have to do this. But the other part of her knew it was the only way to find Georgina and gain justice for her cousin.

The sound of children laughing came from the gated backyard. Meghan caught a glimpse of Irene Mulrooney, the Fitzgerald family housekeeper, picking up Charles's son. A deep longing for a child of her own tugged at her heart. She'd always wanted kids. Her ex hadn't. She hoped maybe one day…

Ryan ushered her inside the house. She heard voices as he closed the door behind them. Others had already arrived. She followed Ryan, barely having time to appreciate the beauty of the wainscoting in the entryway, the intricately carved staircase leading to the second floor or to catch a peek of the antique-filled living room.

The house had been built on a solid foundation and filled with lovely items. She hoped the family was strong like the house to weather this news.

He led her to a high-ceilinged dining room with a long wooden table and a sea of chairs around it, several of which were occupied. She halted just inside the arched opening as everyone in the room quieted and stared.

Trepidation dried her mouth.

She noted with a tiny bit of relief she wasn't the only non-blood Fitzgerald in the room. Pretty, strawberry-blond Merry O'Leary Fitzgerald stood next to her husband, Police Captain Douglas Fitzgerald. The man closely resembled his older brother Ryan. Enough so that Meghan had at one time thought maybe they were twins.

Victoria Evans, Owen's ladylove, and Demi Townsend, the woman who took over nanny duties after Olivia died, were both seated at the table. Meghan liked Demi, they'd become sort of friendly over the past few months. Though Meghan owed her an apology for trying to warn her off Charles. Since he wasn't guilty of any crimes, Meghan was happy that Demi and Charles had fallen in love and recently announced their engagement. They made a cute couple.

Near the window, Nick Delfino, another outsider, took a post, looking forbidding with his arms crossed over his chest. Meghan had only met the former Boston Internal Affairs officer once. He was nearly as intimidating as Ryan. Beside him, Keira Fitzgerald, Ryan's youngest sister, regarded Meghan with a curious stare. Meghan wondered how Ryan felt about his baby sister falling for the man who'd been secretly planted in their department to determine if the Fitzgeralds were legit or corrupt.

Ryan moved away from Meghan to stand near his brothers, Owen and Charles.

Meghan stepped aside to allow Fiona Fitzgerald and firefighter Hunter Reece to breeze past her and enter the room. It was rumored Fiona and Hunter were quite the item of late. Apparently the gossip was true if the way they were holding hands was any indication. Fiona had been widowed two years earlier, leaving her to raise her six-year-old son, Sean, by herself. When an arsonist had recently targeted Fiona's bookstore, Hunter had been the one to save not only the store but Fiona and her son, as well.

"Sorry we're late," Fiona said as she stopped to take stock, her gaze landing on Meghan. "Hi."

"Hi," Meghan managed to croak.

Decidedly uncomfortable at being the focus of so much attention, Meghan edged closer to the doorway. She'd never had a big family. Her father, Phinn Henry, had arrived in Boston from Ireland as a young man and hadn't kept in touch often with his younger sister, Tara, Olivia's mother. Dad had met Mom while working in a brokerage firm. Candice Henry had been an orphan so when Meghan was born it was just the three of them. Until they both died in a car accident when Meghan was twenty-one.

At the head of the table sat Ian Fitzgerald. The current sitting mayor and the clan patriarch. His observant eyes turned Meghan's way. She willed herself to fade into the woodwork. Didn't happen.

A moment later, Aiden Fitzgerald swept into the room, blessedly taking everyone's attention away from Meghan. Tall, distinguished looking, he carried himself with a proud bearing that Meghan had found comforting. Until she'd read Olivia's letter.

Moving to the end of the table opposite his father, he stood facing his family. "I'm sorry to call you here unexpectedly." His gaze raked over the group assembled before him. Regret underscored sadness in his blue eyes. "You all are a part of this family now, so you need to hear."

Anticipation vibrated in the air. Meghan leaned forward, wishing she could claim to be a part of this family. She longed with every fiber of her being to belong to something, to someone. But she was the outsider. That would never change. Because when they learned the truth, they would revile her just as Ryan did.

"As some of you already know, we suspect

Christina Hennessy killed her husband, Burke Hennessy." He cleared his throat before continuing. "And we suspect she may have been involved in the murder of Olivia Henry."

There were murmurs of surprise. Meghan's heart sped up.

"Christina has run off with her adoptive daughter, Georgina," Aiden added.

"You don't think she'd hurt the baby, do you?" Merry asked, her voice laced with concern.

Meghan's own fear reared. Who knew what Christina was capable of?

"I'm hoping not, but we just don't know." Aiden cleared his throat again, apparently having trouble getting his words out. "The truth of the matter is that Olivia Henry was baby Georgina's birth mother."

Meghan heard a gasp, saw the stunned expression on each face.

"Did Christina know?" Fiona asked, her lively blue eyes awash with concern.

"I'm assuming so," Aiden said, his gaze meeting Meghan's briefly.

Meghan noted the grief in his blue eyes. Her fingers curled against the empathy spreading through her.

Tell them, she wanted to scream, but refrained, allowing him time to come clean on his own. But if he didn't say what needed to be said soon, she'd be forced to tell them the truth.

"Now the letter makes sense," Merry interjected.

Meghan blinked. She knew about the letter?

Douglas nodded. "Right. Olivia was writing to her baby not a man as we'd assumed."

Confused, Meghan sought Ryan's gaze.

"Olivia gave Merry a letter before she died," Ryan explained, his voice devoid of emotion. "She'd addressed it to her sweetheart saying they'd be reunited soon."

"Oh." Meghan digested that information. "That supports what she wrote in the letter to me. That she knew her baby was here in Fitzgerald Bay."

All eyes focused on her. All except Ryan who looked away.

"You received a letter from Olivia?" Keira questioned. "When?"

"It was mailed months ago, before she died, but I only recently received it," Meghan said.

"What did it say?" Owen asked.

"Where is it?" Fiona asked.

"Why'd it take so long to get to you?" Charles asked.

Feeling the force of the several sets of Fitzgerald stares, Meghan shifted her gaze to the elder Fitzgerald, willing him to step up and tell the truth.

"I have the letter," Aiden said, drawing his family's attention. He met his father's gaze across the expanse of the long dining table. Ian Fitzgerald nodded ever so slightly. Obviously Aiden had discussed this with the patriarch.

Aiden placed the letter on the table. "There's something I must confess to all of you."

Meghan held her breath.

"Twenty-three years ago I was unfaithful to your mother."

A collective gasp echoed in the stillness of the room.

Charles and Owen didn't look surprised. Meghan saw the slight nod the two brothers exchanged. Interesting. Had Owen and Charles known and kept the information from their siblings? She wondered why.

Meghan's gaze shot to Ryan. A muscle flicked angrily at his jaw. His taut expression tried to mask his thoughts, but the deep, welling pain in his eyes tugged at her heart.

But she couldn't regret bringing the truth to light. Olivia deserved justice for her life and death. Her blood relative, Georgina, was missing. And Meghan needed the resources of the Fitzgerald family to find her.

FIVE

Ryan couldn't take a breath. His world was imploding as he stood in his family home, the one safe haven they all shared, and the only place he'd ever felt truly at peace.

That peace was now shattered into a million fragments that cut his soul to shreds. Everything he'd believed about his father had been stripped away in one devastating blow.

The pedestal he'd placed his father upon toppled. Leaving Ryan feeling vulnerable and uncertain.

Douglas, Fiona and Keira peppered their father with questions. Only Owen and Charles appeared unfazed as they stared at their father with sympathy tempered by anger in their eyes. How could they excuse this? How could they not be reeling the way Ryan was? Unless…

"You knew?" Ryan accused his two brothers. Charles and Owen exchanged a quick glance then nodded. Betrayal sliced through Ryan. "How could you keep this a secret?"

"When did you find out?" Douglas demanded.

Aiden held up a hand. "Please." He waited until his kids had quieted down. "Don't be angry at them. I asked them to let me tell you in my own time and way."

Fury churned inside Ryan. His own time and way? Ha. Like never?

"I know this is a shock and I never intended for any of you to find out like this."

Ryan turned away, unable to look at his father. Nausea filled his stomach, making him regret the eggs and bacon he'd had for breakfast.

"Maureen and I had hit a rough patch. You all were so young. There was so much pressure on me, on her. We were fighting all the time. Your mother and I agreed we needed some distance and time to regain perspective. I went to Ireland for a month."

Each word was like a knife digging deep into Ryan's chest. He remembered when his father took that trip. He'd been gone exactly a month. A long time in a child's eyes. His mother had never once shown distress, always saying dad would be back soon with presents for everyone. And he was.

Ryan still had the chunk of rock claiming to be a bit of the Blarney Stone sitting on his desk as a paperweight. The once happy memory was now tarnished by the truth of what his father had done. Hurt burrowed into Ryan's heart.

"I didn't plan on… I had a brief relationship with a woman there named Tara Henry."

"You mean Olivia's mother?" Fiona asked, her voice shaking.

"Yes." Regret and sadness darkened his eyes. "Olivia was my daughter, your half sister."

"Have you known all along?" Keira demanded. Anger made her cheeks red.

Aiden inhaled and slowly exhaled before answering. "Yes."

Ryan had to give his dad props for not dissembling. "Did Mom know?"

The shame in Aiden's gaze was answer enough. No, she hadn't known. If she had, would she have stayed married to him? Rationally, Ryan understood his father's need to keep his affair and other daughter a secret. He risked losing his family. But he should have thought of that before making such a choice.

Unable to take any more, Ryan headed for the exit. His gaze collided with Meghan's. The sympathy, the pity, on her face was almost more than he could bear.

"Ryan, please, wait!"

His steps faltered. He needed to get out of there. He needed to breath. To think. To ask God why this was happening. How could his father, who professed to be a man of God, do this? Was anyone's faith true? Was his own faith even real?

"I know you're hurt. And you all have every right to be angry with me, but right now we must pull together and find Olivia's child. My grandchild. Your niece."

Meghan laid a hand on his arm, the pressure light, but searing even through his uniform shirtsleeve. "Please, Ryan, you promised to find Georgina and bring her home safely."

Her plea scored him to the quick. A child was in danger, in the hands of a murderer. He'd sworn to serve and protect, regardless of his personal problems. His duty was to find the child.

Compartmentalizing his anger and hurt, Ryan nodded. This was not Meghan's fault. Nor was it the child's. Covering her hand with his, he said, "She is the priority."

Relief flooded Meghan's face. "Thank you."

He wanted to be angry at her, to rail at her for peeling back the veil of deception that revealed his father to be all too human, but he couldn't. She'd acted in the best interest of her family. Just as he would have were the situation reversed.

Now he could only hope to follow her example.

Meghan hovered on the edge of the tight-knit group of Fitzgeralds, overwhelmed by the sheer size and force of the family. The yearning to belong, to be accepted into the inner circle twisted her up in knots. A pipe dream that wouldn't ever come true.

Ryan summed up the events of the past day, including the attempt on their lives.

"Thank the Lord above you're safe," Ian Fitzgerald stated. "This is nasty business. We have to pull out all the stops."

"What we need is to get the public's help," Owen Fitzgerald stated.

Meghan wondered if the detective for FBPD handled fugitive cases often. Fitzgerald Bay didn't strike her as a hotbed of crime. But then again, lately they'd had their fair share of criminal activity. An arsonist, a stalker. Murder. A shiver of dread coursed through Meghan.

"How about flyers?" Merry asked.

"We could put out a press release," Keira said. "Show pictures of Georgina and Christina. I'll volunteer to man the phones for tips."

"I can answer calls, too," Fiona said.

"Me, too," chimed in Demi.

"A press release is a good idea, Keira," Aiden said with approval in his tone.

The rookie police officer and youngest of the Fitzgerald children beamed.

"But a press release will only hit the surrounding area," Douglas pointed out. "We need national coverage since we have no way of knowing how far Christina has taken Georgina."

"A press conference, inviting all the stations in the state, would be the best way to reach a wider audience," Nick said.

Aiden nodded. "I agree. I'll make a plea to the public."

"Are you sure that's a good idea?" Fiona asked. "I mean with the mayoral elections coming up. If the public finds out about your…our family's connection to Georgina, it could hurt your chances of winning the election. Maybe you should let Ryan be the spokesperson on this."

"With Burke Hennessy dead, there's no question Dad will win the election," Owen stated. "No one in their right mind would vote for Judge Monroe, not with how he helped cover up what his son was doing."

"That's for sure," quipped Keira, her blues eyes flashing with anger.

"There's no proof he covered anything up," Douglas said.

"And it's not fair to think people wouldn't vote for the judge because his son went bad," argued Demi.

Charles moved up behind her and placed his hands protectively on her shoulders. "I agree with Demi on that."

"Exactly why I think Ryan should take the lead on this," Fiona said.

Meghan watched the interplay between the siblings with interest. The love they shared was evident even in their arguing. And she appreciated that they all had a voice and weren't afraid to speak up.

"Aiden, it's of course up to you," Nick said, pushing away from the wall. "But I agree with Fiona that keeping you out of this would be better all the way around. We need the public looking for Georgina and Mrs. Hennessy, not distracted with another scandal."

"Granddad would be the better choice to talk to the press," Ryan finally spoke up. Though nothing showed on his face, Meghan detected the note of unresolved anger in his tone.

Looking like he'd aged in the past half hour, Aiden nodded. "You're right, of course. Dad?"

Ian Fitzgerald rose. "I'll have my secretary set it up." The patriarch ambled from the room.

"We'll need photos of both Georgina and Christina Hennessy," Nick said.

"I can get those," Keira offered.

"In the meantime, we need to keep searching for Christina," Douglas said.

"The BOLO hasn't yielded anything," Owen said.

"What about family? Christina's parents?" Victoria asked.

"We haven't found any so far," Ryan said. "But we'll keep searching."

"I have an idea," Meghan said and winced at how small her voice sounded.

All heads turned toward her. She cleared her throat. She kept her gaze on Ryan. "If I hadn't found Helen at home, my next stop would have been to the town of Belmont to the Elm's Peace Center to see Dr. Bates."

Ryan tilted his head. "Explain."

"Dr. Bates was her psychiatrist."

"How did you find that out?" Charles asked.

Meghan glanced at the town doctor then back to Ryan. "People talk."

Ryan's mouth pressed together. Then he nodded. "I'll contact the doctor." He turned and walked out of the house.

For a moment Meghan stared at the empty doorway. Then she swung her gaze over the Fitzgerald clan. No one said a word, but they didn't have to. The looks of distrust, of curiosity, spoke volumes. Her gaze landed on Aiden.

He held Olivia's letter in his hand. "You should go with him, Meghan."

His quietly said words sent surprise sliding through her but she didn't take the time to analyze why he'd want her to accompany his son. She whirled around and raced out of the house.

Ryan had just started the engine on his SUV. She jumped into the passenger seat.

"What do you think you're doing?" he demanded.

She clicked the seat belt in place. "Coming with you."

"No."

"Yes."

"Get out."

She shook her head. "Not going to happen. Look, Ryan, I'll only follow you. We might as well work together."

"I'd rather work alone."

"I wouldn't." The admission was out before she realized the truth in the words.

She'd been operating alone for so long, she didn't understand why she now suddenly needed a partner. The image of the men in the van tore through her mind, the sound of the bullets hitting the car, the blood from where she'd been hit brought fear screaming back into her system. There was a very good reason to stick close to Ryan. Safety. She wasn't a fool. And dying wasn't on her To Do list anytime soon.

"You may not need me," she said, "but I need you. What if the masked men in the van find me again? Or you, for that matter? We don't know who they were after or why."

His scowl darkened. "All the more reason for

you to stay in town. Go home, Meghan. Let me do my job."

"I can't. Georgina is my relative, my blood. I have to find her. I won't stop until I do. So you'll have to forcibly remove me from your car. But that will take time. Something you don't have to waste right now."

His lip curled. For a moment she thought he might force her from the vehicle, but then he threw the gear into Drive and stepped on the gas. "Stubborn woman," he muttered.

She sat back and released a tense breath. She'd been called worse.

Meghan Henry shouldn't be riding with him, tagging along on a police investigation. He gripped the steering wheel until his knuckles turned white. This went against department standard operating procedures.

Okay, they did have a ride-along program, but still… She was an unauthorized civilian. And a reporter. Two strikes against her. Oh, wait, there was a third—she'd just upended his world.

"Tell me what you've heard about Christina." Ryan's side throbbed, reminding him that a mere twenty-four hours ago he'd been engaging in law enforcement's version of mixed martial arts. Didn't matter. His injuries were a nuisance that had to be endured. All that mattered now was tracking down Christina, arresting her for murder and securing Georgina.

The tires of his SUV burned up the pavement on the way to nearby Belmont, a town west of Fitzgerald Bay. He cut through the parade of cars with one eye on the road and the other on the rearview mirror, keeping vigilant for any suspicious cars or vans following them. He didn't want a repeat of that event. He didn't have to see Meghan's shoulder to feel badly that she'd been grazed by a bullet on his watch.

"I'm not sure how reliable the information is," Meghan said, "but apparently Christina had a history of mental illness and suffered a nervous breakdown several years ago. She'd been hospitalized in a neighboring town under the care of a psychiatrist."

Great. With a history like that, who knew what the woman was capable of? He slanted Meghan a quick glance. "Who told you this?"

"Townspeople," she said. "It was the word on the streets. So to speak."

He'd done his fair share of interrogations over the years, so he knew what extracting information from a suspect was about. But getting ordinary people to open up to a badge wasn't an easy task. People tended to be wary, suspicious even, regardless that they'd known Ryan since he was a baby. Yet they spill their guts to the nosy reporter? "I don't get it. Why? Why do people open up to you?"

She shrugged. "I asked the right questions when I'm buying my coffee, standing in the checkout line at the market or ordering my lunch. Half the job of being a reporter is getting people to talk. You get them to relax, to talk about familiar things, mundane things, eventually leading them to the gossip you know they're dying to reveal."

He snorted. "Small-town gossip isn't usually without some embellishment."

"Are you always so cynical?"

Ignoring her question, he changed lanes. The woman annoyed him. Not only because she'd been the catalyst to throwing his family back into scandal and rocking them to the core, but she was brash and a know-it-all type and would probably not think twice about endangering her life and those around her. He'd seen her in action.

His mouth twisted. He didn't want to like her in any way. But he couldn't deny the grudging admiration filling his chest at the way she'd fought for Georgina. Add brave and courageous to the list of her faults.

Stay focused, he told himself. "Let's hope the doctor has some useful information."

When they arrived safely at Elm's Peace an hour later, a well-dressed woman escorted them through a nicely decorated lobby toward an office. She gestured for them to enter.

"Dr. Bates will be with you shortly."

"Nice place," Meghan commented and moved to the window overlooking a flower-filled courtyard. A few people of various ages wandered the paved path cutting through splotches of green grass and flower beds.

Ryan didn't care about the aesthetics of the facility. His thoughts centered on finding Christina Hennessy and the little girl. He swallowed hard. His niece. An image of the toddler's bright eyes tore through his mind. She had the Fitzgerald blues, just like his siblings and him. A trait handed down by their father. Georgina's grandfather.

Anger stirred in his chest but also protective instincts, so ingrained in his blood he didn't question them. To protect and serve strangers was one thing. Georgina shared the same blood that ran through his veins.

And Meghan's.

His steps faltered.

Meghan shot him a glance. He looked for a crack in the tile floor behind him.

The door opened and a tall, sandy-blond-haired man entered. He was younger than Ryan had imagined he'd be, considering his profession. "Dr. Bates?"

"Yes, and you must be Deputy Chief Fitzgerald." Bates held out his hand.

He had a firm handshake. Ryan could tell a lot about a man by his handshake. Too tight, the guy was trying to prove something. Too loose, meant insecure or hiding something. Firm, but not crushing, spoke of confidence. Trustworthiness? Had to be proven. "I spoke to your nurse on the phone. I assume she told you why we've come."

Bates turned his attention to Meghan as she stepped forward, her hand outstretched with a business card. "I'm Meghan Henry, freelance journalist."

The doctor read the card. The smile he sent her was just shy of a leer. Ryan clenched his jaw shut to keep from telling the guy to back off. "Miss Henry. My pleasure. Interesting to have law enforcement and a reporter in my office at the same time. A dichotomy to be sure."

The flare of interest in the doctor's eyes as his gaze took in Meghan made Ryan's fingers curl. She did look pretty with the sunlight streaming through the window at her back, kissing the golden highlights in her hair. Her hazel-green eyes snapped with intelligence as she assessed the doctor in return.

Bates turned back to Ryan. "I'm sorry, Deputy Chief, but you do understand I can't tell you anything without written consent by my patient."

"Christina Hennessy is still an active client, then?" Meghan asked.

Bates frowned and shot her a glance. "I didn't say that."

Ryan's mouth twisted at the corner. No, he hadn't, but it was implied. Ryan had no doubt Christina would use her mental status and her association with the doctor to her advantage when arrested. "Do you have any idea where Christina Hennessy would go?"

Bates shook his head. "Even if I did I couldn't reveal the information to you."

"Did she have any visitors while here?" Meghan asked.

"Really, Miss Henry. HIPAA laws prevent me from revealing any information whatsoever. I'm sure you understand."

Meghan fired off, "But a child is in a dangerous situation. Aren't you obligated to talk to the authorities?"

Bates heaved a heavy sigh. "I would have had to have seen Christina with the child."

A fire built in Meghan's eyes.

Ryan stepped closer to Bates. He had a couple inches on the guy and used every millimeter. "Listen carefully, Doctor. Christina Hennessy is a suspect in two murders. She's armed and dangerous. She's on the run with her adoptive daughter. If anything happens to that child, you'll have to live with the knowledge you could have saved her, but chose not to."

The doctor stepped back, his complexion slightly green. "I can appreciate the gravity of the situation. But you must understand my hands are tied. Legally."

"Please, Doctor," Meghan said. "The little girl is my cousin. I have to find her before something bad happens to her."

Sympathy pooled in Bates's eyes. "I wish I could help you. I'm truly sorry."

Meghan's gaze whipped to Ryan. "Get a court order."

He nodded. "It'll take time."

With her mouth pressed into a tight line, Meghan bolted from the room. Ryan's heart squeezed tight with unexpected empathy. His own frustration gnawed at him. With effort he unclenched his hand to give the doctor his card. "Call me if you change your mind or think of something that would be helpful without breaking patient confidentiality."

Bates took the card with a nod.

Ryan hurried out the door. He expected to find Meghan in the entryway but she was nowhere in sight. A flash of worry knotted his gut. He frowned. She'd probably gone to wait by the car. He strode toward the exit. His bum ankle gave him grief with each step. A flash of honey-blond hair caught his attention. Meghan was standing in the courtyard talking to an older woman who kneeled at the flower bed to pull weeds. A moment later Meghan came inside, excitement danced in her eyes.

Grabbing his arm and practically pulling him toward the door, she said in a low voice, "Christina has an aunt who visited her a few times while she was in the facility."

Admiration for her tenacity and ingenuity infused him. The woman wouldn't let anything stop her from her goal. He only hoped her determination wouldn't be her downfall. Or his. "Who told you this?"

They pushed through the door and stepped back into the sunshine. "Mrs. Hargrove. She's been a resident patient here for over ten years. She remembered Christina. They'd played bridge together."

"How did you know to ask her?" Ryan asked, impressed by her ability to ferret out information.

She made a flippant gesture with her hand. "She was the second patient I asked. Lucky break."

"You work fast," he commented as he opened the passenger door for her. "Do you have a name and an address?"

"Just a name. Dosha Meniski."

At least they had that. It was a start. Something for them to go on.

Them.

He shook his head in bewilderment. When had he started thinking of them as a team? He should be the one having his head examined.

SIX

Ryan punched the name *Dosha Meniski* into the national database on his computer. They'd returned to the Fitzgerald Bay police station and headed straight for Ryan's office. He sat at his desk, and Meghan paced the short length of floor from the window to the door and back. Ryan's gaze strayed to her as he waited for the information to appear on the screen. She really had nice legs. Long and toned. He'd seen her out running on the beach several times over the past few months.

The computer dinged. He forced his gaze away from her legs and back on the screen. A file appeared.

A Dosha Meniski resided in Brookline. He knew the area, made up of mostly Russian immigrants.

"What did you find?" Meghan asked.

"An address. Not sure it's the right person, but worth checking out," he replied as he hit Print.

"Can we go see her now?" Meghan asked, coming to a halt at the edge of his desk.

Ryan rose and took the paper the printer spat out. He wanted to tell her he'd go alone, but knew that would only cause an argument because the tenacious Meghan wouldn't be benched. She'd only insist on tagging along. Or would follow him as she'd threatened to do before. Since time was of the essence, he said, "Let's go."

Twenty minutes later they arrived at a block filled by an apartment building on a tree-lined street. They quickly found the correct apartment number on the fifth floor. He knocked. The door eased open.

Putting a hand up to halt Meghan from entering, he withdrew his weapon and pushed the door wider. "Dosha Meniski?"

No answer. Fearing the woman might be injured or worse, Ryan said to Meghan, "Stay here."

He entered the apartment, dreading and half expecting to find another crime scene. He quickly went from room to room looking. No one was home. All seemed in order. He holstered his weapon and returned to the front room.

Meghan had stepped inside the spotless living room, except for the child's toy sitting in plain sight on the plaid couch.

"Don't touch it," Ryan said just as Meghan gasped and rushed to pick it up.

He groaned with irritation.

"This is Georgina's," she said. "I've seen her with this baby doll before."

Letting go of his exasperation because they *were* making the sort of progress that made his blood hum, he said, "Doesn't mean Christina brought her here recently."

Meghan stared at a group of framed photos on the mantel. He stepped closer. One was of a group of children, all dressed up. The boys wore suits making them look like little businessmen. The girls wore black-and-white fancy outfits. Some had aprons on over their dresses.

One picture stood out. A lone smiling girl of around seven or eight years old. She wore a black-and-white jumper with a ruffled white blouse beneath and her white-blond hair was parted into two high ponytails. He pointed to the huge white puffy bows on top the girl's head. "Those are some fancy doodads."

"They're traditional in Russian and Ukrainian cultures on the first day of school, which is a huge production in these countries called First Bell. The kids dress up like it's prom night. It's quite fascinating. They take their education very seriously."

"How'd you know that?"

She shrugged. "I've traveled some. I think this is Christina as a little girl. Did you know she was from Eastern Europe?"

He hadn't. He'd always assumed she'd been from Boston or the vicinity. He looked back at the picture, really studying it. In the background behind the little girl, a white banner hung across a yellow block structure. The letters on the banner made no sense to Ryan. "Is that Russian?"

"Or Ukrainian. They're similar enough that I have trouble remembering which is which. I'm not fluent in either."

"Excuse me," a sharp voice called from the doorway. "What are you doing?"

Ryan spun around. A plump woman stood just inside the open front door. "Are you Dosha Meniski?"

"No. I live next door." The woman's gaze flickered over Ryan's uniform but her posture didn't relax. "Is Dosha in trouble?"

"That's what I'm trying to find out," Ryan said, moving closer. "Have you seen her recently?"

"She was here last night with her great-niece and great-grand-niece. But I haven't seen them today."

Ryan's heart sped up. Not a dead end after all.

"Does Dosha own a car?" Meghan asked, her voice tinged with excitement.

He admired her quick thinking in asking the question. He seemed to be doing that a lot lately.

"A red Cadillac. It's not parked in its usual spot though."

Ryan clutched Meghan by the elbow and steered her toward the door. "Thank you so much, ma'am." He paused to offer the woman his card. "If you see Dosha, please have her call this number."

They left the building.

"She was here," Meghan said. "We've got to find them."

"We will." He started to dig in his pocket for his phone to call the Boston precinct who did have jurisdiction here so they could get to work.

A loud crack split the air. Gunfire!

Meghan cried out as bits of sidewalk cement puffed up mere inches from her legs. Pulse rocketing, Ryan reacted instantly, yanking Meghan down behind the back bumper of his SUV. The shot had been angled from an elevated trajectory. The shooter had the advantage of higher ground. Ryan glanced around the bumper, looking for the sniper on the building across the street. There, on the far west corner of the roof, he could just make out the silhouette of the gunman.

Not good.

In a low crouch, Ryan scuttled backward until he could open the rear passenger door. "Get in," he ordered Meghan. She dove inside. Another round pinged off the hood of the vehicle. Ryan winced, hoping the engine hadn't suffered, too, and opened the front passenger door and slid inside and across to the driver's seat.

The back window exploded. Glass flew into the SUV, shards making it all the way to the front seat. Meghan let out a startled cry.

Ryan worked to get the key in the ignition. "You okay?"

"Yes. Get us out of here!"

"Working on it," he muttered.

The engine roared to life. Slouched down so he could barely see over the dashboard, he threw the gear into Drive and gunned it. The SUV shot forward with a squeal of rubber on road. Another bullet hit the back fender. Ryan yanked the steering wheel and took the corner, putting a building between them and the shooter. He sat up and headed toward the highway.

Taking out his cell with one hand, he called Boston P.D. and reported the shooting. Were they being followed? Or had someone been waiting in case they showed up at Dosha Meniski's apartment?

Only one person knew they were headed to Dosha's—the patient at Elm's Peace. Unless someone *had* been following them. He was positive there hadn't been a tail on the way to Meniski's.

But someone could have put a tracking device on his rig.

Obviously the attempts made on their lives had to be connected with Christina and Georgina. He was beginning to seriously doubt Christina, the lawyer's widow, was the boss of all this. Though how it all connected, he didn't know. He glanced at Meghan, her hair covered in glass from the back window, her eyes wide with panic twisted him up inside.

He better find out fast.

Before someone else died.

Meghan tried to breathe. In. Out. But fear continued to shake her to the core, making the simple task of taking in air difficult.

She sat up straight in Ryan's SUV and buckled the seat belt around her. Air swirled through the now-shattered back window, whipping her hair into a frenzy. Much like terror was whipping her insides.

She clasped her hands together to regain control.

"Someone sure doesn't want us poking around," she managed to say. Her voice sounded like a cartoon mouse. All high and squeaky.

"That's an understatement," Ryan replied, meeting her gaze in the rearview mirror. "You're not hurt?"

"No. You?"

"Not this time."

Everything had happened so fast she hadn't even had a chance to pray before Ryan had hustled her into the car. He'd saved her, protected her. He was strong and capable and every inch the hero she'd needed him to be.

She lifted up a prayer of thanksgiving.

Dear Lord, thank You for protecting us. And thank You for Ryan. For making him the man he is. Please show us how to find Georgina. I beg of You, Lord. Don't let any harm come to her.

Ryan's phone chirped. He answered, listened for a moment then said, "I'm on my way in."

After he hung up he said, "Granddad's press conference just aired. The tip lines are going nuts."

A jolt of anticipation made her sit forward. "That's good, right? Someone has to know where Christina and Georgina went." *Oh, please, oh, please.*

When they arrived back at Fitzgerald Bay police station and entered the building, Douglas Fitzgerald clapped Ryan on the back. "Glad you're here in one piece, brother." Douglas turned his sharped-eyed gaze to Meghan. "Miss Henry, no worse for the wear, I see."

She managed a smile and picked a shard of glass from her hair. "A little shaken."

Douglas nodded. "Comes with the territory."

"News?" Ryan asked.

"Lots of supposed sightings of Christina Hennessy and the little girl. California, Florida, downtown Boston. We're following the leads as best we can."

"We have a lead, too," Ryan stated. Meghan and Douglas followed him into his office.

"Christina's great aunt has a car," Meghan explained.

Douglas gave a nod of acknowledgment then turned to watch his brother. Meghan did, too. Her pulse quickened.

Ryan's handsome face was a study in concentration. His blue eyes intent on his task. He punched the keys on his keyboard, his mouth set in a grim line. Nothing that had just happened seemed to affect him. All business, no worry. No *what ifs*. She admired that about him. Wished she could be more like him in that way.

A moment later he turned the monitor so they could see the document on the screen. "A red 1996 Seville Cadillac. License number TLX 596."

"Sweet," Douglas said. "I'll get a BOLO out on it ASAP."

After his brother exited, Ryan rose and came around the desk. "You should go home now and rest. You look like you're about to fall over."

She shook her head, hating the way the world seemed to have shifted. She was tired and a little light-headed, but her pride wouldn't let her admit as much to him. If he could keep going, so could she. "No way. I'm staying the course on this."

"Then you at least need to eat. Keep up your strength."

"Only if you join me." She wasn't letting him out of her sight. He'd probably take off on a lead while she had her face buried in a plate of spaghetti. Which sounded really good. Her tummy rumbled. Ryan's soft laugh made her cheeks burn.

He brushed away a stray strand of hair from her face. "I could use some refueling, too."

A shiver of awareness shimmied down her spine at the slight touch of his warm skin. The sensation was unexpected and pleasant and a bit frightening.

Ryan gestured for her to lead the way out of the office. Needing some distance to collect herself and cool the attraction sizzling in her veins, she walked out of the station, careful to keep an arm's length between them as they headed down the street to the Sugar Plum Café and Inn. The quaint restaurant was owned by Victoria Evans, soon to be Mrs. Owen Fitzgerald, and looked like something out of a Norman Rockwell painting.

White porch with lattice railing, rocking chairs filled with content patrons sipping iced tea beneath hanging baskets teeming with colorful early summer blooms. Meghan sighed, sounding a bit wistful even to her own ears. In fact, the whole of Fitzgerald Bay was straight from Rockwell's imagination, or so Meghan theorized.

Her own rented cottage by the sea was something from a fairy tale. Quaint and cozy were words that sprang to mind.

She didn't look forward to leaving her cottage or Fitzgerald Bay. But she would eventually have to return to Boston and the life she'd had before her cousin's murder. She didn't belong in Fitzgerald Bay. No matter how much she wished she did.

They entered the wide foyer of the Sugar Plum with its quarter-sawn oak woodwork and glass pastry case full of delicious-looking treats that made Meghan's mouth water. And added inches to her waist just by being in the same vicinity.

Victoria Evans descended the antique staircase leading up to the guests' rooms. Her heeled shoes made no sound on the floral runner. Her anxious gaze searched their faces. "Did you find Georgina?"

"Not yet," Ryan said.

Disappointment and worry knitted her brows and clouded her eyes.

"But we have more clues to follow," Meghan stated, wishing the clues would hurry up and bear fruit.

Victoria nodded. "This is so stressful for everyone." She turned her attention to Ryan. "Owen feels just awful for keeping his father's secret from you."

Ryan made a slight scoffing noise in his throat. "I'm sure Owen will get over his guilt quick enough."

Victoria's eyebrows dipped. "I know how hard hearing the truth was for you and your siblings. You have to understand Owen was dealing with his own issues, too."

Meghan knew Victoria referred to the daughter she'd kept hidden from the Fitzgeralds for nine years.

Ryan's jaw tightened but he didn't respond.

Feeling the need to diffuse the uncomfortable situation, Meghan said, "We'd like a table, if one's available."

Victoria motioned to the hostess. "Charlotte will seat you."

They nodded their thanks and followed the older woman to a table in the corner. Dusk was fast closing in. The setting sun hung low on the horizon, a brilliant burst of orange and gold against a backdrop of blue sky and water.

After they'd perused the menu and ordered, Meghan eyed Ryan warily. He sat angled toward the window, his face in profile, his blue eyes staring intently at the ocean beyond the shoreline.

The man was a paradox, at times gruff and domineering. Yet there was a tender, humble side that occasionally showed itself. She wasn't sure what to make of him. Or what to think. He was so different from her ex-husband on every level. She was attracted, no question. Respect and admiration for Ryan had embedded themselves firmly in her mind and heart. Empathy made her want to reach out to him. Fear of what he could do to her heart kept her still.

Growing uncomfortable with the silence and giving in to the urge to draw him out of the hurt she knew had to be eating at him, she ventured, "I appreciate how hard you're working to find Georgina and bring my cousin's murderer to justice."

His gaze slid to her. "I'm doing my job."

She wasn't buying his act. This had become personal for him just as it was for her. "True, but considering the circumstances, you're doing your job well."

He scoffed. "We'll see."

"I'm sure your father appreciates it, too."

"I don't want to talk about my father," he said, his voice tight with anger.

"I don't blame you for your anger. I'm angry, too. One would think the chief of police would have more honor and integrity."

Ryan's gaze snapped to her face. He opened his mouth then clamped his teeth together so hard she heard the crack and wondered how he didn't break a tooth. No doubt he reflexively wanted to defend his father.

Unaccountably, she felt badly for Ryan that he couldn't. His father's actions were indefensible. Seeds of hostility and resentment burrowed in, trying to find moist ground.

Aiden Fitzgerald had had a hand in Meghan's cousin's death, even if he hadn't struck her with the rock that delivered the fatal blow. Olivia had gone to him for help and he'd turned her away. Left her to fend for herself because he'd been too spineless to face the consequences of his long-ago actions. Not to mention his candidacy for mayor.

Where was the forgiveness? The grace and mercy?

God's word said she needed to forgive those who hurt her. She knew the passage by heart. Had resisted the instruction for so many years. Her heart throbbed as conviction dug deep, clawing at old wounds she'd hoped had healed over.

But letting into her heart even the tiniest bit of bitterness scraped at the scars left on her soul by her ex-husband's abuse, reminding her of the battle she'd faced and overcome.

The road to forgiveness was long and narrow and fraught with thorns. But, oh so freeing.

Her giving over to anger and fueling Ryan's hurt and rage only made her part of the problem not part of the solution. She needed to be Ryan's help just as Nurse Justine had been for her that day in the hospital when she'd nearly died from the injuries David had inflicted.

Though why she felt compelled to reach out to Ryan Fitzgerald she didn't know.

Well, okay, so she did know. She liked him. Liked his integrity, liked his protectiveness and the way he cared about her, his family, his job. He was a man of action, a man of his word. He put duty ahead of his own hurt and that said a lot about his character. And made him dangerous to her peace of mind because she could easily see herself falling for him. *So* not a good thing.

Yet, she couldn't let him suffer.

Meghan reached across the table to lay her hand over his. The contact sent heat curling up her arm. "I'm sorry. That comment was uncalled for. I have no right to judge your father or his actions." She remembered the anguish in Aiden's eyes as he had confessed his fallibility to his family. That hadn't been fake. "I'm sure he's hurting just as you are."

"I don't understand him." Confusion and pain etched lines in his handsome face.

For an unguarded moment she glimpsed the turmoil going on inside Ryan and her heart ached for him. "We all make bad decisions sometimes, horrible choices that have far-reaching consequences we can't anticipate or want."

"That's an understatement." He looked away, his jaw set. "It's one thing to keep his affair secret all these years. But another to keep quiet about Olivia, especially after she came to town."

"In his misguided way he was trying to protect all of you," she said. But not his illegitimate child. A spark of anger flared. She battled down the flame to a smoking ember.

He stared at her, his disbelief as clear as glass. "How can you be so forgiving?"

Drawing on her faith and the wise words a kind nurse had once told her, she said, "Forgiveness is a process. Taken step by step. Moment by moment. Consciously giving over to God what we can't humanly do ourselves. Forgiveness is the way to freedom from that which binds us." And if she recited the words often enough, she'd finally master the concept. She hoped.

Ryan's mouth twisted. "Trite words meant to offer comfort no doubt, but how could you possibly understand the depth of betrayal I feel?"

Defensiveness rose. "I know how devastating the cut is that you feel all the way to the quick of your soul when someone you love, someone you trust turns on you." She'd given her heart so easily, so foolishly only to have the man she'd married beat her to a pulp. Literally.

"Who hurt you?" Ryan's voice softened. He turned his hand over to twine his fingers with hers.

She swallowed, realizing too late she'd unwittingly opened up a door she wasn't ready to pass through with him. "We're not talking about me. I'm trying to help you."

"But I'm not allowed to return the favor?"

She swallowed and was grateful to see the waitress heading over with her arms ladened with their dinner.

The smells of rich marinara sauce wafted from the plate of pasta. Meghan reached for a slice of garlic bread in the breadbasket at the same time as Ryan. He pulled his hand back. "After you."

Appreciating his manners, she took a piece. Hoping to keep the conversation from turning back to her, she said, "The Red Sox are playing the Orioles tonight."

He arched an eyebrow. "You a baseball fan?"

"You can't live in Boston and not be." She took a bite of her spaghetti. Her eyelids closed as she savored the taste. There was nothing better than pasta sauce done right.

"Good, huh?"

Her eyelids flew open. "What?"

He watched her with an amused gleam in his eyes. "You looked like you were enjoying your food."

"I am," she said and took a drink of iced tea to cool the burn of embarrassment heating her checks. "Is your Stroganoff good?"

"Yes." He twirled some of the flat noodles covered in creamy mushroom sauce and held it up. "Want a taste?"

She nearly choked on the bit of bread she'd put in her mouth. Tasting each other's food was an intimate act shared by close relations or…people in relationships. She was neither.

And had no plans to travel down that road.

SEVEN

"So what do you think of the Red Sox this season?" Meghan asked, her gaze on the bread she was tearing to pieces, the crumbs landing in a pile on her half-eaten serving of pasta.

Her words about forgiveness echoed in Ryan's head. His curiosity about her deepened. Someone had hurt her. From the background check he had done on her—after the first time she'd stormed into his office demanding to know what he was doing to find her cousin's killer—he knew Meghan was divorced. He could only guess that the marriage had ended badly.

He wanted to go back to that conversation, find out more about her, but he had the distinct impression she didn't. Ryan, too, had memories he couldn't bear to think about. Memories that spread the pain of being disillusioned through him. Keeping the evening light probably was for the best. He had so much turmoil going on in his brain right now, he was struggling as it was. "I think they'll make the play-offs."

"Did you play baseball growing up?" she asked.

"Yep, all the way through high school. But I was better at basketball. It was more fun. A faster game."

A smile played at the corners of her mouth. "I like basketball, too. I played in junior high."

"I can see you playing basketball. You should stop by the community center some time for a pick-up game." She had an athletic grace about her. She was tall for a woman, lean, but with curves in all the right places. He blocked *that* thought. Noticing her figure was not a good move under the circumstances.

Keep it professional, Fitzgerald.

He couldn't let his guard down because this woman held the power to devastate his family.

Apparently done with her attempt at conversation, she lapsed back into silence and finished off her meal.

He studied the contours of her face, liking the high cheekbones and the soft pout of her lips. What made her tick? If he understood her better, maybe he'd find a way to convince her to keep the information about his father from going public. "Did you grow up in Boston?"

She startled as if he'd poked her. "Oh, yes. Yes, I did. Born and raised in the same neighborhood where my mother grew up. My dad immigrated to America from Ireland as a young man when he was twenty years old. He met my mom not long after, and they were married three weeks later."

Ireland. The country of his forefathers, who'd immigrated to America in the 1800s and settled Fitzgerald Bay. Meghan's ancestry, too. And Olivia's country.

Hurt reared at the reminder of his father's fall from grace. He viciously subdued the pain, forcing it back to the cramped box in his soul. "You're an only child?"

"Yes. I always wished for a brother or sister, but…" She shrugged. "I envy you having so many siblings."

He thought of Douglas's concern after they'd been shot at. "They're the best. I'm the oldest. The responsible one. Mom expected me to keep the others in line, back then and now." He gave a small dry laugh. "As a kid, I resented each baby who arrived—one more sibling to take the attention."

"I imagine that's normal," she said.

"Maybe. But no matter how hard I tried not to care for each new baby brother or sister, I would always fall for them." He shrugged. "I couldn't help myself when they stared up at me with big eyes as if I were their entire world."

He trusted his siblings implicitly. He'd lay down

his life for each one of them without a heartbeat of hesitation.

He'd yet to meet anyone outside the family who inspired the same sort of trust and devotion. Oh, he'd dated, but never seriously. There always seemed to be something…missing.

His sister Fiona, the sensitive book lover, often lectured him that he didn't give any woman enough of a chance and one day he'd regret it. He couldn't conceive of losing control enough to open his heart.

"I can't envision having such a big family," she said. "It was always just Mom and Dad and me. Now it's just me. They died in a car accident."

The grief in her tone stirred an echo of empathy and understanding in his heart. His mother had been gone for years, but the loss was as fresh as if it were yesterday.

"I'm sorry."

"Me, too."

His cell phone chirped. He checked the number then answered, listened as he scooted his chair back and hung up. "We need the check," he called to the waitress.

"What's happened?"

Anticipation revved in his blood. "The BOLO on the Seville got a hit in Manhattan."

Meghan scrambled out of her chair. "Then New York, here we come."

"Not tonight. We'll meet at the station first thing in the morning. I'll make arrangements for us to take the first flight to New York. The NYPD can take care of it for now."

"But—"

He held up his hand. "Nothing can be accomplished if we're dead on our feet. Tomorrow will be soon enough. Besides, we don't know if this is a real lead or another dead end."

Worry clouded her pretty eyes. She bit her lip, something he'd noticed she did when nervous or scared. For a short time they'd managed to put the anxiety and fear aside. Now it slammed back into place. He could only hope they found Georgina tomorrow and arrested Christina. He wasn't sure how much more of this Meghan could take.

Nor why her well-being mattered so much to him.

After escorting Meghan to his father's house to retrieve her rental car, he'd followed her to the beachside cottage she rented. He'd made sure the place was secure before beating a hasty retreat, needing to put some distance between them.

His emotions were running high. His attraction to Meghan messed with his judgment. Not a combination that bode well for success. He had to get a grip. Keep things in perspective. He'd been delivered an emotional blow. A child was missing, a murderer on the loose and they had only one lead.

Instead of heading to his own home just down the beach from Meghan's, Ryan went back to the police station. The place was well lit. He waved to Jackson who sat at his desk drinking coffee, waiting for a call on this quiet night.

From his office, Ryan made the necessary flight arrangements to New York for him and Meghan.

His brother Douglas appeared in Ryan's office doorway. "Hey, I thought you left."

"I did. Now I'm back."

"You heading to the Big Apple in the a.m.?" Douglas asked, stepping fully into the room.

Ryan ran a hand through his hair. "Yeah. Taking Meghan with me since I know she'd just follow me anyway."

"You could lock her up," Douglas suggested with a sardonic grin.

"Believe me, I've thought about it." Ryan leaned back in his chair. "The woman's become the bane of my existence."

Douglas hiked a hip on the edge of Ryan's desk. "You got it bad."

Ryan shot straight up. "What? No." *Maybe. Oh, man.* He wasn't sure how he felt. He hadn't wanted to get close, to like her. Or admire her. Or care about her. But he did. He liked her. Admired her. And, yeah, he'd started to care.

Douglas snorted. "I've watched the way you two have danced around each other for six months. Now you're practically joined at the hip."

"Not my doing," Ryan snapped, feeling thoroughly cranky now.

"Right." Douglas shook his head. "You know, she's a good-looking lady. Smart, too. And stubborn."

Ryan eased back again. "You got that right. Stubborn doesn't even cover it."

"You should bring her to Charles and Demi's engagement party. She and Demi know each other."

Ryan had forgotten about the upcoming celebration. Charles and Demi had become inseparable after Charles helped take down Demi's stalker. Now he was going to make her his wife and the kids' mom. They made a good couple. Complemented each other. Ryan was glad his brother had found some happiness after the heartache of his ex-wife's abandonment.

He scowled. Bring Meghan? To a family function?

Hmm. Maybe if he included her, gave her a chance to know his family and came to care about them, she'd be less likely to go public with his father's duplicity.

But bring a date? No, it wouldn't be a date. He wasn't ready for that. It would be a strategic move meant to protect his family. It wouldn't mean he and she...they were a couple.

"I'll ask her. After we get Georgina back and put Christina behind bars." He pinned his brother with a hard look. "But it's not a date."

Douglas's knowing grin burned a hole through Ryan's conscience. "You keep telling yourself that."

True to his word, the next morning Ryan was waiting for her when she arrived at the police station. He still had on his uniform.

"Did you get any sleep?" she asked. Her own night had been fraught with nightmares of guns and car chases.

"Some. There's a cot in the back room," he replied, running a hand over his stubbled jaw. "Hang tight for a minute. I'll be right back."

Meghan watched him disappear down a hall.

The knot that had formed in her chest last night when he'd asked her who'd hurt her had lessened slightly, but the tension in her shoulders hadn't let up. Their dinner together had been congenial once the food had arrived. By tacit agreement they'd stayed away from the topic of his father and her revealing words. She'd enjoyed hearing how he felt about his family, his siblings. And though talking about her parents always brought a pang of sadness, talking to him was surprisingly easy.

In the light of day, she wasn't sure what had transpired between them last night. But whatever it was didn't matter. They had a lead on Georgina. Meghan might be holding her only living blood relation by nightfall and her cousin's murderer would be in jail.

Dear Father in Heaven, please reunite me with Georgina.

Ryan returned with only the slightest bit of a limp, reminding her of the danger. Anxiety formed a lump beneath her breastbone.

He'd shaved and changed into civilian clothes. Well-worn jeans that looked good on his long, lean legs. A button-down dress shirt, open at the collar and rolled up at the sleeves. In his hands, he held two black flak vests with the words *Fitzgerald Bay Police* emblazoned across the chest and a small black case with a lock. Her anxiousness ratcheted up a notch.

"Any chance I could convince you to stay behind?" he asked, his blue eyes searching her face intently.

"No way."

His mouth twisted at the corner. "Didn't think so." He handed her a vest. "Just in case."

The heavy weight of the body armor slammed home how precarious the situation had become. But they were in this together. Partners.

She hoped that neither of them found their heads in the crosshairs of sniper fire. Again.

The plane touched down at JFK International Airport with a smooth glide along the tarmac. The engines revved as the reversers deployed. Impatience had Ryan unbuckled and poised to grab the bag with the flak vests from the overhead bin before the flaps on the wings let down.

Meghan remained motionless in her window seat. Her mouth pressed tight, her gaze trained on the seat back in front of her.

"You should have told me you were afraid to fly," he said.

Her hands had a death grip on the armrests. "I managed."

Yes, she had. His respect for her grew. The plucky woman hadn't blinked or given any clue that she'd battled with aerophobia when he'd handed her the plane ticket. She was an enigma.

Bold and brash at times, yet every so often, like now, he glimpsed a vulnerability that touched him. And earlier, when she'd spoken of betrayal and hurt, he'd sensed and seen the anguish she carried deep inside.

A welling need to soothe and comfort rose till it became a painful ache in his chest.

Someone had her hurt badly.

Rage at the unknown person filled him. He

could only hope Meghan suffered nothing more serious than a broken heart.

Not that he was dissing the pain of having one's heart smashed to smithereens. He'd had his fair share of heartbreak. Who hadn't? But there were worse hurts, which left scars that he marveled ever healed.

The memory of another young woman rose, making his already-stretched-tight nerves strain even more. Ryan had witnessed his best friend assault a girl he'd professed to love when they were in high school. Ryan had intervened and then turned in his friend to the police even though the girl refused to press charges.

The decision still lay heavy on Ryan's psyche but he didn't regret doing the right thing. And he knew that Lily Wilkin was grateful, even if she refused to speak to him, claiming doing so hurt too much, brought back the nightmares. He understood. He'd had his share of nightmares from that day.

He could only pray that Meghan's hurts weren't nearly as horrific.

The plane jerked to a halt at the gate. Once inside the terminal, dodging travelers pulling rolling luggage, they weaved their way through the crowded airport. After retrieving his locked gun case from baggage claim, they headed outside to the taxi stand. Once they climbed into the yellow sedan, Ryan gave the address of where Dosha Meniski's Seville had last been spotted.

As they wound their way into the city from the airport, Ryan pulled out his cell and checked in with the NYPD. Captain Gregson of the 13th precinct said he had an officer waiting for Ryan outside the apartment building where the car had been spotted. He spoke a moment longer, then hung up his phone.

"Have they seen any sign of Georgina?" Meghan asked.

Her anxiety sizzled in the air around her.

"No. But if they see Christina, they'll detain her and take Georgina into custody," he said, not sure how to lessen her anxiousness. He needed her to be ready for whatever came at them.

Meghan's straight white teeth tugged at her bottom lip. She clutched the large nylon bag he'd stuffed the flak vests into and stared out the taxi's side window.

"It's going to be okay."

She gave him a wan smile. "Thanks for saying so."

They lapsed into silence. Hoping to get her mind off her worries, and because he was curious, he revisited their unfinished conversation at the Sugar Plum. "You never answered me."

Her eyebrows arched. "Oh? I don't remember the question."

He didn't believe that for a second. The woman was smart and on top of it like nobody's business. He thought back to what she'd said about getting people to open up. Getting them talking about the familiar, the mundane, leading them to the words they were waiting to say. Good strategy. Would probably work better than his more straightforward, go-for-the-throat approach. Ask the right questions, she had said.

He wondered what question he should be asking. "Do you really believe forgiveness is possible?"

Surprise flickered in her hazel eyes, then settled into determination.

She did remember. He'd thought so.

"Yes," she answered. "Like I said, it takes time."

"A lifetime," Ryan stated, thinking it would be that long or more before he could let go of the anger and hurt over his father's infidelity and duplicity.

"Maybe" she said. "But it's so much better than the ugliness. The soul-sucking nastiness that burrows in and eats away at you until you convince yourself death would be better than living."

He blinked. *Whoa. Where was this talk of death coming from?*

The stress, the tension of being shot at and terrorized, no doubt.

Tread slowly, Fitzgerald, he told himself, suspecting they were approaching a special place of trust where she might actually open up. And that touched him.

But then again, judging by the shuttered look closing over her expression, he could be wrong. "I'm sure my dad would like me to forgive him and have everything return to the way it was before..." He swallowed the words before they were spoken.

"Before I came barging into your office with the truth," she finished for him.

He gave a dry laugh. "Yeah. Something like that."

"Life will never go back to what it was, but that's okay. The past is over and done with. Now you have to figure out how to live in the now, then the future. And trust me when I tell you, finding it within yourself to forgive is the only way each day becomes bearable."

"For me or my dad?"

She tilted her head in thought for a moment. "Both of you. But you mostly, since you're only in charge of yourself, your emotions." She shifted to better face him. Her lovely face held him in rapt attention.

"Forgiveness is for you," she continued, seeming to warm to the subject, making him think she was speaking from experience. "Forgiveness releases the icky stuff so you're free to love. To be in a relationship with God, with others."

"What if I can't release the icky stuff?" he asked, wondering what icky stuff she'd had to release, to forgive.

"Holding on to the bad feelings only hurts you," she answered, her hazel eyes imploring him to understand what she was telling him. "Not the one who hurt you. They don't feel any of what you're feeling. We each only know our own pain, joy, hurt, anger, sorrow. We can empathize, we can have compassion...."

Her mouth kicked up slightly at the corner in a wry grimace. "At least healthy, well-adjusted people can. But only you can choose to forgive. The cliché 'Let go and let God' is a cliché for a reason."

"Here we are," the cabdriver said as he pulled the yellow sedan to the curb.

Ryan almost regretted the intrusion. He helped Meghan from the cab, her words ringing in his head and rattling around his heart.

Forgiveness releases the icky stuff.

He certainly had a good dose of icky going on.

The address in New York turned out to be a low-rise walk-up apartment in the East Village on Avenue B. The area once referred to as Alphabet City in its seedier days, now looked to be getting a face-lift as several of the brick, prewar structures had scaffolding crawling over them like locusts.

Ryan hadn't been to this part of the city in years, not since he and his college buddies had haunted the Big Apple on the weekends. They'd covered every square inch of the island on the lookout for the best places to eat. Food was a big deal when you're a growing young man in college.

The smells of a noodle house offering soy-sauce-ladened dishes mixed with the more commercial scents wafting from a popular Tex-Mex restaurant next door made Ryan's stomach rumble. The plane's muffin and coffee hadn't been enough of a breakfast.

Hip and trendy stores replaced the old tattoo parlors and punk-rock shops that had once catered to the more bohemian crowd. One of Ryan's buddies had gotten a tat at a shop several blocks down.

What had brought Christina to this neighborhood?

A police cruiser sat parked at the curb. A young uniformed police officer stood casually on the sidewalk. He nodded to an elderly woman passing by. Ryan approached him. He read the name tag on the officer's shirt. "Officer Cribs."

Cribs snapped to attention with a wary look in his eyes. "Yes."

Ryan showed him his badge and introduced himself and Meghan. He showed the officer the photos he'd brought with him, flashing the images of Dosha Meniski, Christina Hennessy and Georgina Hennessy.

The officer shook his head. "No one's come out or gone in since I arrived."

"We'll have to go door-to-door," Ryan stated and helped Meghan don the flak vest.

She grimaced as the weight of the jacket dropped onto her shoulders. "Is this really necessary?"

"Considering we were shot at yesterday? Yeah, necessary."

"Okay then."

He approved of her attitude, appreciated her spunk. She might need that and more depending how things turned out. He unlocked his gun case, palmed his service weapon and chambered a round before tucking the Sig into the holster clipped to his belt. "Can I stow this in your trunk?" Ryan asked holding up the case.

"Of course." Cribs popped the trunk. Ryan tossed the case inside.

"Captain Gregson said I was to accompany you," the officer said, falling in step with them.

Ryan nodded, glad for the support. They entered the building and started knocking on doors, showing the three photos to the residents. The building was old, but clean.

The stairwell was muggy and hot. Ryan's cotton shirt stuck to his back. On the fourth floor,

Meghan paused to tie up her hair, exposing the graceful lines of her neck.

On the top floor of the five-floor walk-up, they encountered a bent old man who studied the photos before pointing down the hall. "There. Apartment F."

Adrenaline pumped through Ryan's veins. He pulled Meghan behind him. He and Cribs flanked the door. Holding his Sig Sauer in a two-handed grip, with the muzzle pointed down, Ryan allowed Officer Cribs to take the lead.

Cribs rapped his knuckles against the prefabricated door. "NYPD. Open up."

No sounds came from inside the apartment. Ryan's gut clenched. He glanced at Meghan. Her apprehensive expression ramped up his own anxiety. He remembered the way Meghan had prayed after Christina escaped with Georgina. Though his faith was on unsteady ground, he sent up a silent request. *Lord, let us find Georgina and capture Christina. Keep my little niece safe.*

Abruptly the door swung open, startling Ryan. He pointed his weapon at the woman standing in the doorway.

EIGHT

Short, round and *weathered* were the words that sprang to Ryan's mind. A real old-world babushka, complete with a triangular scarf covering her graying hair. His gaze searched beyond the woman. The apartment appeared empty.

"Are you Dosha Meniski?" Cribs asked.

"*Da.* I am Dosha," she answered, her voice heavily accented with the distinct sound of Eastern European descent. "Finally you come."

Confused, Ryan lowered his weapon. "Is your great-niece Christina here?"

Dosha shook her head, worry pinched the corners of her eyes. "No. I'm worried. She's not in her right mind."

Behind him, Ryan heard Meghan's soft intake of breath. She pushed past him to face Dosha. "Where's Georgina?"

Dosha wrung her hands. "She go with Christina." Her gaze pleaded with them. "Please, you must help. I fear for the baby."

Frustration added weight to Ryan's heavy heart. He holstered his weapon. "Do you know where they went?"

The young officer eased past them and quickly made sure the small apartment was indeed empty save for Dosha.

"No. Christina received a phone call. Then she bundled baby up and took her. I plead with her to leave little girl with me, but she wouldn't. She told me to say goodbye to Georgina. I worry she won't be back."

Ryan's mind raced with possibilities. Something at the periphery of his thoughts clamored for attention.

"Christina didn't take your car," Meghan said.

"I watch from window. She climbed in a taxi. I don't know where they were going. The taxi headed uptown."

He clasped her hand. "Thank you."

They left Dosha with the promise to let her know when they found Georgina and Christina. He would find them. No matter what it took.

Outside on the sidewalk, Officer Cribs called his dispatch. Within moments they had the name of a cabdriver and current location for the taxi that had picked up a fare in front of the East Village apartment building.

Officer Cribs drove them across town. As they sat at a stoplight, Ryan glanced out the passenger window. The building on the corner was a bank that reminded Ryan of the anonymous package they'd received not long after Olivia's death. The box had contained a baby blanket and hospital bracelet tipping them off to the fact that Olivia had given birth to a baby girl. They never had discovered who'd sent the package. Ryan had a sickening feeling in the pit of his stomach that he knew who had sent the items in hopes they'd led to Georgina.

His father.

Welling rage and bitterness crashed over him, making him clench his jaw until it ached. Meghan's words chased along behind, *Choose to forgive.*

Right now he couldn't.

But he also couldn't give in to the fury wanting to spill out. He had to concentrate on the immediate need. Georgina. Her safety was paramount. Bringing in Christina ran a close second.

He refocused, replaying the contents of the package in his mind.

In addition to the baby items, the box had contained an uncashed check in the amount of ten thousand dollars made out to Olivia. Drawn on that bank in New York signed by a William Sharp. The account was closed and the lawyer's address had turned out to be bogus....

More frustrated than not, he struggled to put

the pieces together. Had this check been a pay-off by the Hennessys? Or a payment for the baby Olivia had given up? Why hadn't Olivia cashed the check?

Who was this lawyer and what part did he play in the death of Olivia? Was there a connection between Sharp and the Hennessys?

He blew out a breath as the questions battered at his mind like baseballs spitting from an out-of-control pitching machine.

They found Christina's taxi driver leaning against his car and eating a hot dog on Broadway.

Officer Cribs hung back as Ryan approached the man. He wore a Yankees ball cap backward, jeans and a short-sleeve loose shirt. Mustard smears on his cheek stood out in sharp contrast to his dark skin.

"You Ajay Baboor?" Ryan asked as he stepped close, blocking the guy in.

Wariness flickered in his dark eyes. "That's me. Who wants to know?"

The heavy Brooklyn accent surprised Ryan. So much for stereotypical ideas. "I'm Deputy Chief Ryan Fitzgerald." He showed his badge. "You picked up a fare this morning. A woman and child."

"These two," Meghan said, holding up the photos they'd brought of Christina and Georgina.

Ajay glanced at the photos then his gaze darted between Ryan and Meghan. "Yeah. So?"

"Where did you drop them off?" Ryan pressed.

"Was the little girl okay?" Meghan asked, her voice betraying her anxiety with a slight tremor.

Ajay nodded. "Yeah, the kid was great. Laughing and chattering up a storm. Mom wasn't so happy, though. Kept telling the kid to shush." He shook his head. "Some people don't get that kids are kids and can't help their babbling. I see it all the time."

"But where did you drop them off?" Ryan repeated his question.

"The 500 block of West 178th, up in Washington Heights."

Another lead to follow. Ryan felt like he was chasing after Hansel and Gretel. At least Christina had left a trail of crumbs in her wake. "Did you make any other stops?"

Ajay nodded. "Sure did."

Meghan stepped forward. "Where?"

"You're not a cop," Ajay observed, his gaze raking over her with interest.

Ryan glared at the man, not liking they way he leered at her.

"No, I'm not law enforcement," Meghan said. "I'm a reporter and that little girl is my relative."

Ajay frowned fiercely. "Kidnapped?"

"Yes," Meghan said. "Any information you have could help us."

With a nod, Ajay said, "Picked up a suit on West 47th. Snappy dresser. He had even less tolerance for the toddler than the woman."

Meghan made a noise that expressed the disgust Ryan felt. "Did you catch the guy's name?"

Ajay shook his head. "No. But they were meeting someone and the suit was anxious because they were running behind. Gave me an extra twenty to 'step on it.'" Ajay snorted. "Give me a break. Twenty bucks will hardly buy me lunch let alone get me to violate traffic laws." He raised his chin in acknowledgment of Cribs.

"Can you describe the man in the suit?" Meghan asked.

"White. Five-ten, brown hair, brown eyes. Navy pinstripe with a red-and-yellow-striped tie. Like I said, snappy dresser. My guess the guy was a lawyer of some sort. You know how *they* are."

Ryan took it the guy didn't have any more of an affinity for lawyers than he did cops. "Anything else?"

Ajay shrugged. "Nope. That's it."

"Thank you," Meghan said and hurried toward the awaiting cruiser. Ryan followed closely behind. Officer Cribs expertly maneuvered through the thick New York traffic, slowly working their way farther uptown.

More questions poked at Ryan. Was this lawyer the same one who had issued the check to Olivia? If so, then how were he and Christina connected?

The 500 block of West 178th was a busy intersection with access to US 1 and I-95 crossing over Harlem River Drive and flowing into the Bronx.

The buildings were defaced with gang graffiti. Piles of black garbage bags sat on the sidewalk. The stench of refuse hit Ryan immediately as he climbed out of the cruiser. A group of teens eyed them warily before dispersing in different directions. He was thankful for the marked car.

"Now where?" Meghan asked, her gaze wide as she looked around.

A metal door of the nearest building rolled up and a man hefting a full garbage bag strolled out and plopped the bag on the curb, adding to the growing mound.

Ryan held out the picture of Christina, figuring she was striking enough to have drawn notice. "Have you seen this woman recently?"

The guy grunted and shook his head before disappearing back inside.

"Of course, that would have been too easy," Ryan commented wryly.

"Nothing about this has been easy," Meghan said.

"Too true. Let's start hitting the doors."

Fifteen minutes later, a boy of about seven recognized Christina's picture. "She went in there." He pointed to a brick building with boarded-up windows.

"What would she be doing in there?" Meghan murmured. "That doesn't look like a good place to bring a child."

No, it wasn't. But given Christina had no problem with guns and thugs...

Ryan's senses went on high alert as they approached the building. Cribs led the way inside the dark, dank entryway. The smells of urine, decay and burnt cabbage permeated the air.

"Ugh." Meghan held her hand to her nose and mouth.

The loud retort of gunfire erupted overhead.

Heart jumping and training kicking in, Ryan drew his weapon and pulled Meghan behind him. Cribs grabbed his radio off his belt and reported in. "Shots fired. Second floor." He spouted the address before taking a position by the rickety-looking elevator.

"Aren't we going up?" Meghan asked as she huddled close behind Ryan.

He wasn't taking any chances with her safety. "No. We'll wait for backup."

A door at the end of the hall banged open and three people came charging out of the stairwell.

Ryan instinctively drew Meghan back even as

his mind registered that he was facing Christina Hennessy and two men. The trio banked right and disappeared down another hallway, obviously seeking to escape.

Meghan must have seen them as well because she burst out of his grip and ran full speed after them. Fearing for her safety, Ryan closely followed as one thought slammed into him, knocking the breath from his lungs.

Three people. Three adults. His stomach sank. His chest tightened.

Where was Georgina?

A strong hand grabbed Meghan by the collar of the heavy flak vest weighing her down and jerked her to a stop. She yelped with surprise and frustration. She whipped around to find herself brought up short against Ryan's chest, made thick by the vest he wore.

"Hey, they're getting away," she protested. The back door of the building banged shut behind the trio. A horrifying realization worked its way into her consciousness. "Georgina hadn't been with Christina!"

Where was she? Was she safe?

The sounds of sirens announced their backup had arrived.

Ryan pushed past her and barked out a command as he went. "Stay put."

He charged ahead, disappearing out the same back door that Christina and her posse had fled through.

Two police officers raced toward her.

"That way!" she instructed, waving in the direction Ryan had gone. "Hurry!"

Breathing hard from adrenaline and fear, Meghan raced to the elevator. Cribs had gone to the building's front door to greet the officers. She entered the elevator and pressed the button.

"Miss Henry!" Cribs called out just as the elevator doors slid shut.

Her mind worked through what had just happened. Shots had been fired. Christina and the two men had escaped. Ryan had gone after them. Georgina had to be still inside the building.

She stepped out of the elevator onto the second floor landing. An apartment door to the right stood wide open. The smell of gunpowder lingered in the air. Heart pounding in irregular beats, Meghan rushed forward even as dread sent icy tendrils curling down her spine.

She stepped into the apartment. The coppery scent of blood assaulted her senses, triggering her gag reflex. A man's body lay sprawled on the living room's threadbare, ugly brown carpet. Dark ribbons of blood stained his once white shirt from what appeared to her untrained eye to be two bullet holes in his chest. Her own chest ached in an empathic response.

Tearing her gaze away from the horror of the deceased man, she searched for any sign of Georgina. There were boxes full of passport folders, a computer and camera sitting on a scarred old table. A dirty kitchenette was at the other end of the room. The messy bedroom and bath were empty. Her gut clenched. Where was Georgina?

"Miss Henry, we haven't cleared the building yet. This is a crime scene. You gotta stay out of here." Officer Cribs came to her side, trying to drag her away from the macabre sight.

"Georgina? Have you found her?" Meghan asked, panic making her voice reedy.

"No. There's no sign of the little girl," Cribs answered, applying more pressure on her arm, compelling her to leave the apartment.

In the dimly lit hallway, Meghan grabbed his shirtsleeve. "You have to find her. She has to be here, in the building, somewhere."

The panic gripping her took away all her composure. She could hardly think straight.

He nodded. "We'll search for her. But you must stay out of the way."

Frantic with worry and dread, Meghan forced herself to breathe to keep from hyperventilating. She had to find her. Where could Christina have taken Georgina?

Meghan's gaze landed on the door to the stairwell. Christina and accomplices had come through it on their way to escaping.

Hoping against hope to find her sweet relative, Meghan yanked open the stairwell door and stepped inside. She peered over the railing, but saw no sign of the toddler on the descending or the ascending staircase.

Nearly overwhelmed with disappointment and anguish, she went back to the first-floor landing. Her heart leaped into her throat as Ryan escorted Christina into the building with her hands cuffed behind her back.

Ryan's gaze, full of hope, met Meghan's. Tears burned the backs of her eyes as she gave a negative shake of her head. His expression darkened, his jaw firming.

Meghan stepped in front of Christina, blocking the path. "Where is she? What have you done with her?"

"You," Christina ground out. "You've ruined everything."

"Please, Christina," Meghan pleaded as Ryan handed Christina over to another NYPD officer's custody. "Please, tell me where she is."

"Excuse us, ma'am," the officers said.

Ryan gently applied pressure at her elbow. She received the message loud and clear. The officers needed her to move out of the way so they could escort their suspect from the premises. She turned on him. "You can't let her leave until she tells us where Georgina is."

"We can talk to her at the police station," he said. His tortured expression mirrored what she felt inside.

Reluctantly she stepped aside. A leaden weight bowed her shoulders as Christina was escorted out of the building.

"What happened to the men?" she asked.

Ryan ran a hand through his hair, his fingers leaving grooves in the thick, dark strands. "They escaped. An NYPD officer gave chase, but…"

"Do you know who they were? What were they doing here? Did they say anything to help us find Georgina?" Hysteria simmered blow the surface, making her voice shake. She wanted to find Georgina so badly she felt physically ill.

"No," he replied and walked toward Officer Cribs's cruiser.

She raised her stinging gaze to the sky. The situation kept getting worse. How much more could little Georgina take? How much more could she take?

Four days ago it had all seemed so simple. Find Georgina, get her to safety and sue for custody. Simple. Only, life was never simple. Nor easy.

She'd learned that lesson long ago. But God

never promised it would be easy or simple, only that He would be there for her to cling to.

And cling she would because that was all she had to see her through this nightmare.

There were times when Ryan completely understood the vigilante mind-set. This was one of those times. He'd never entertained thoughts of harming a suspect in custody before, and he hated feeling the burning need to shake Christina Hennessy's tongue loose now.

The woman refused to talk after her outburst when she'd seen Meghan. A smart move on her part. Aggravating for Ryan.

Standing against the back wall of the NYPD interrogation room, he pinned Christina Hennessy with his most intimidating glare. Gone was any semblance of the icy social-climbing wife of a prominent lawyer. Christina's blond hair was matted with sweat and dirt, her clothes filthy from running through the back alley. Her right shoe missing, lost somewhere during the chase.

Captain Gregson, a behemoth of a man with thinning hair and a steely gaze, sat across from Christina at the metal table in the interrogation room of the 13th Precinct.

The bad lighting made the woman's complexion pasty with a yellow tint.

Ryan glanced at the two-way-mirror wall to

his right. Meghan sat behind it watching, hoping Christina would confess to murder and reveal Georgina's location. It gave Ryan a measure of comfort knowing that Meghan would be praying as she surely was. Her faith was strong. Hopefully, strong enough for them all.

Because the rage burning inside Ryan wasn't very Christian-like.

Ryan had cornered Christina against a chain-link fence while her partner in crime had scaled the barrier. Ryan had been tempted to rough her up a little. Anything to find out the location of the missing child.

And the fact that she was at a known forger's hidey-hole only added strength to his suspicions that Christina was guilty. Of exactly which crimes, he had yet to determine.

The dead man in the apartment was a notorious forger. Christina wouldn't say who killed the man. The other two unidentified suspects were in the wind.

Ryan eyed the cup of water Christina primly drank from, unwittingly leaving behind her DNA. At least by the end of the day they'd have the evidence needed to run against the unidentified DNA found on the rock that had killed Olivia. Ryan had little doubt the two DNA samples would match, confirming Christina's involvement.

But that wasn't what had his gut twisted in knots.

Georgina was still missing. He prayed the child was alive.

Ryan couldn't take Gregson's tactic of waiting Christina out any longer. He removed the photo of Georgina he'd been carrying in his shirt pocket and laid it on the table in front of Christina.

"Do you love her?" he asked quietly.

Christina's gaze dropped to the picture. Georgina's face beamed at the camera. Her bright blue eyes danced with merriment. Her chubby little cheeks puffed up in a wide grin. The child looked happy, healthy. Well cared for. Loved.

The stony expression Christina had maintained since the moment he'd apprehended her shifted, softened. But she remained stubbornly mute.

"Do you love her?" Ryan pressed, hoping to reach the woman's maternal side, the side that had wanted a child desperately enough that she'd adopted one. Or bought one. No matter what it took, Ryan would dig into the adoption and uncover the truth after he rescued Georgina. "She loves you."

Christina winced, giving Ryan hope that he was getting through.

A sharp rap on the interrogation room door made Ryan's stomach clench with frustration at the interruption. He was so close to getting what he and Meghan needed.

Gregson slid from the chair and opened the door. He stepped out into the hall.

Ryan took the vacated seat and pushed the image of Georgina closer to Christina. "You went to a lot of trouble to bring this little girl into your home, into your life," he said quietly. "You're her mommy. You've taken very good care of your daughter. She needs you now more than ever. She's scared and alone, needing her mommy."

Her eyes welled and a single tear fell and landed on the table with a splat.

Glad to see some emotion in the woman besides anger, he pressed, "Tell me where she is so we can help her."

NINE

The door to the interrogation room burst open and a man in a tailored suit marched in with Gregson following close behind.

"I'm Mrs. Hennessy's attorney, William Sharp. You have no right to question my client without my presence," Sharp said as he came around the table to stand beside Christina.

Ryan whipped his gaze to Gregson.

Gregson shrugged. "He's her lawyer."

Ryan's fingers curled into fists. Just how had the lawyer known to show up? Christina hadn't asked for him. He turned back to Christina. The tears had dried.

"I'll tell you what you want to know if you let me go," she said, her voice hollow.

"Christina, don't say a word," Sharp commanded. "I'd like a moment alone with my client."

Anger made the nerve in Ryan's jaw tick. The rules said he had to acquiesce. He glared at Sharp a moment before meeting Christina's gaze. He had to give it one more shot. "She needs her mommy. Wherever she is right now, she's scared and doesn't understand why her mommy has abandoned her."

"Really, Captain," Sharp said to Gregson. "Control your lackey."

Ryan's nostrils flared at the insult but he kept himself still.

Gregson's hand fell onto Ryan's shoulder. "Come on, Fitzgerald, we have to give them their moment."

Despairing that what little ground he'd managed to gain with Christina would be lost forever if he left the room, Ryan made one last desperate play. He made a show of rising to his feet. "If you cooperate, I'll talk to the D.A. I'll see what kind of deal we can make."

"Enough," Sharp barked. "She has rights and you're violating them."

Ryan held up his hands in a show of surrender, but his gaze never left Christina. "She's been read her rights. She doesn't have to talk to me if she doesn't want to."

She picked up the photograph and stared at the image. "You talk to the D.A., come back with a deal and then I'll tell you where to find her."

"It doesn't work that way." Glad she was continuing to dialogue with him, he said, "You've got to give me something to take to him."

Sharp leaned down until he was even with

Christina. "I can get us out of this," Sharp insisted. "Just stop talking. You know what will happen to us if you don't."

Finally they were getting somewhere. Ryan fought not to react with obviously excitement. They have a boss.

"Who are you afraid of?" he asked.

Neither said a word.

"We can protect you," Ryan offered, needing them to spill.

Again, silence.

Hoping that changing the focus would eventually lead them back to Georgina and to their mysterious boss, Ryan said, "Tell me, Christina, why did you kill Burke? He loved you."

Sadness darkened her expression. "Poor Burke. He blamed himself because we couldn't have children."

"You wanted Georgina," Ryan pressed. "You wanted a child."

She nodded. "We had tried for so long to have one of our own. But it didn't happen. So Burke contacted William. They had worked together years before. William said he could get us a child."

"Christina, you're killing me here," Sharp snapped. "Be quiet!"

She ignored his outburst. "All we had to do was fly to Ireland and pick her up. We didn't ask questions. At least not then. We thought it was legal."

She frowned. "I thought it was legal. Apparently, Burke knew it wasn't."

"My client is under a great deal of stress and doesn't know what she's saying. I demand a moment alone with her," Sharp said, his voice betraying his panic. "Now."

"If she wants it," Ryan said, keeping his gaze locked on Christina.

She seemed to have reverted inward, her gaze unfocused on the photo in her hand.

"When that woman showed up, claiming to be my baby's mother, I couldn't believe it," she continued as if Sharp hadn't interrupted her. "How had she found us? Why did she want my child? She'd given her up. Thrown her away."

She turned accusing eyes on Sharp. "That's what you told me. You said she was a drug addict. That she'd sold you her baby so she could do more drugs." She shook her head. "That wasn't true. She wasn't an addict. She was just a scared young woman who'd thought she hadn't any other choice. Because you and Roman convinced her of that."

Roman, Ryan registered. Another name to add to the list of players

Fear contorted Sharp's features. "I only told you what you needed to hear. She agreed to give up her baby. No one coerced her. And she was paid handsomely for the child."

Ryan briefly wondered if the lawyer realized he'd just confessed to the illegal practice of baby selling. Human trafficking.

"Who's Roman?" Ryan asked, sensing a piece to this puzzle was about to snap into place. "Is he one of the men who ran away? Your boss?"

"No. He's no one," Sharp said, cutting the air with his hand. "A figment of a demented mind. Mrs. Hennessy suffers from a mental illness. We have documented proof."

Not surprised by that play, Ryan returned his attention to Christina. He'd come back to this mysterious Roman later. "Olivia came to you, wanting to regain custody of her baby."

"Don't answer that," Sharp warned, a note of desperation lacing his words.

"Yes. But I wouldn't give Georgina up. And Burke was afraid Olivia would go to the police," she said. "He couldn't allow that."

She had. She'd come to Aiden Fitzgerald, her father, for help. And he'd refused to believe her. Anger churned in Ryan's soul. He pushed it into a deep, dark compartment to be dealt with later. "So Burke killed her?"

Her gaze snapped to his. "Yes. Yes, he killed her. He didn't want his chances of being elected mayor to be ruined."

Surprised, Ryan made a mental note to check Burke's DNA along with Christina's against the evidence. "But Burke didn't declare his intent to run until *after* she'd been killed."

Christina blinked, her gaze shifting slightly. "He'd been planning to run for a long time."

Since Burke wasn't here to defend himself, Ryan could only rely on the evidence to tell them the truth on Olivia's murder. For now he'd go with this scenario. "Okay. So Burke killed Olivia to keep her quiet. Then why did you kill Burke?" he asked again.

She drew back. "I didn't," she said, maintaining the stance she'd taken from day one. "I found him. Dead." Her voice rose in near hysteria. "My Burke. I found him."

"I demand you stop interrogating my client," Sharp said. "You're upsetting her."

Ryan softened his tone. "Christina, let's stay focused on Georgina. Where did you take her? She needs you now."

"My baby." Christina appeared on the verge of unhinging. Her eyes grew wide as horror spread over her face. "He took her. He's going to sell her again. You have to stop him. You have to stop them."

"Who, Christina?" Ryan pressed. "Who is Roman and what does he have to do with Georgina?"

Sharp stepped closer in an attempt to block Ryan. He glared at Christina. "You say any more and we're both dead."

* * *

Meghan strained forward, nearly pressing her nose against the glass of the two-way mirror. Her heart pounded in her throat as anticipation wound her nerves into knots. So close. They were so close to finding out where Georgina was. She willed Christina not to listen to Mr. Sharp. Willed her to sacrifice her own well-being for the child she'd brought into her life.

Meghan had every confidence Ryan would be successful. He had to be.

Christina clutched Ryan's hand. Meghan held her breath. She wished she could be holding his hand, sharing his strength. She'd come to rely on him. To care about him. He was a good man. Fair, honest. He hadn't disappointed her. She hoped, prayed, she wasn't making a mistake in trusting him.

"You have to find Georgina before it's too late," Christina pleaded. "I should have never given her back. They'll sell her to someone else. Someone who won't love her, who won't care for her the way I did. What have I done?"

A muscle jumped in Ryan's jaw. Meghan knew he was trying to rein in his impatience and frustration. His self-control was something she appreciated and respected about him. A trait she wished to emulate because she was having trouble keeping her own anxiety from causing her to break through the glass and put her hands around Christina's throat.

Someone had Georgina and they intended to sell her. Georgina could be lost forever.

Oh, Ryan, please, get the info we need.

As if sensing her plea, he glanced toward her. Though she knew he couldn't see her through the mirrored glass, she felt his touch all the way to her toes. Her heart squeezed tight.

Come on, come on, Meghan silently urged as each tick of the clock drew Georgina farther away. Where was Georgina?

Ryan swung his attention back to Christina. "Give me a location."

Christina frowned. "I don't know. They took her away." She swung her gaze to Sharp. "But you know where she is."

"She's irrational. Don't listen to her," Sharp said, desperation reeked with every word.

"Tell them where they took her," Christina screamed.

He shook his head. "You may have a death wish, but I don't."

"What makes you think they don't already presume you've talked?" Ryan asked, his voice hard and uncompromising.

If anyone could get the information, it was him.

Her respect and admiration for him tripled. He was a special man. A man worth allowing into her heart.

Sharp clamped his mouth tightly shut. Christina jumped up from her chair and flew at Sharp with her fingernails out like claws. Sharp yelped and tried to defend himself against the attack by covering his head with his hands and cowering. Ryan and Captain Gregson pulled Christina off the lawyer.

"Tell them!" Christina screamed as she continued to lash out at the air. "Tell them about how you broker sales. Tell them about the babies!"

Meghan's reporter's antennae rose high. Baby smugglers? Human trafficking. She'd been right. Christina had been into something a lot bigger than they'd imagined. Just how involved was she? She acted as if she were an innocent victim in all this but, if that were the case, then why run away with Georgina in the first place?

Sharp ran a hand over his jaw. "You've done it now."

Ryan planted his feet wide and faced Sharp. He looked like a warrior ready to do battle.

"You're both in way too deep," Ryan said. "The only life preserver you're going to get is if you cooperate and tell me who and what."

"You'll provide me protective custody?" Sharp asked, his face taking on a haggard appearance.

Funny how he didn't include Christina in the bargain.

Ryan exchanged a glance with Gregson who gave a single nod. "Yes. Now tell me where the child has been taken."

Sharp's shoulders sagged beneath his designer suit. "All I have is an address in Queens."

"It's a start," Ryan said.

Meghan ran for the door, praying with everything in her that this time they would be successful in their search for Georgina.

A little girl's life depended on it.

The address in Queens the lawyer Sharp had given to Ryan turned out to be a rickety two-story house built in the '20s. Dormer-style windows jutted out of the second floor roof like warts on a hag's nose. Shutters hung off rusted hinges.

The place appeared deserted. The overgrown lawn needed a good mowing and the flower beds housed an abundance of weeds. No parked car to indicate a resident. All the window coverings were drawn closed and the high chain-link fence encircling the yard was meant to keep out unwanted intruders, not to keep a cute puppy dog or child contained.

But looks could be deceiving. Who knew what they would find inside? Hopefully, Georgina.

Antsy anticipation infused Ryan as he prepared himself to join the tactical team stationed at the end of the block. A white van sat parked at the curb, its back door open. Men donning flak vests hovered nearby, ready to invade the structure that supposedly housed a baby-smuggling ring.

Ryan broke away from the van to talk to Meghan. His heart softened when he saw her. She sat in the passenger seat of Cribs's cruiser at the end of the block with a view of the back of the house and alley—her pretty lips pursed in annoyance. He understood how she felt. It was never fun being sidelined when you wanted to be a part of the action. He appreciated that she hadn't put up a fuss when Officer Cribs had driven her far enough away that she wouldn't be in danger.

He leaned down to look into the open passenger window. "You okay?"

"I will be once you get Georgina," she said, her gaze meeting his.

The trust, the confidence in her gaze made him more determined to fulfill the promise he'd made to her. "It won't be long now. You stay here, no matter what."

She frowned. "Meaning?"

He hated to scare her any more than she already was, but she had to know how dangerous this situation was. "This could get ugly. I doubt the men who have Georgina are going to come willingly or quietly."

She arched an eyebrow. "In other words, if I hear gunfire I should duck?"

Liking her pluck, liking her, he nodded. "Exactly. I'll send Cribs back to stand guard."

"I'm safely tucked inside this car. I'll roll up the window and lock the doors. Let Cribs help. You need all hands on this."

Maybe, but her safety was his responsibility. He wouldn't let anything bad happen to her. Would never forgive himself if she got hurt. She'd come to mean a lot to him. More than he'd ever thought possible. He'd never intended for that to happen. But it had. No, Cribs would be returning. Ryan didn't want to be worrying about Meghan when he needed to be concentrating on Georgina.

"I promise I won't do anything stupid," she said, as if sensing his thoughts. "If I got in the way and something happened to Georgina because of me…"

"I'm not going to let anything happen to her," he assured her.

"I know."

Her confidence warmed him. He tapped the door. "It's time. See you in a few."

"Ryan." She reached out through the window and grabbed his hand and halted him from leaving.

"Yes?"

Concern lit up her lovely hazel eyes. "Please be careful."

She cared. About him. The realization sent his blood pulsing. "You're worried about me," he said in a little bit of awe.

She tugged him closer. "Yes, I am. Please, promise me you won't take any chances."

"I promise." He closed the distance between them to place a light, gentle kiss on her sweetly shaped mouth.

She inhaled sharply, a quick breath that stilled his.

He felt the surprise on her lips. He drew back, unsure of her reaction. Unsure of his own. Had he overstepped the bounds of their... He was loath to qualify their association as a relationship. Yet...

Her fingertips slowly rose to touch the spot where he'd kissed her. Color heightened the contours of her cheekbones.

His ego puffed up. Were her lips tingling like his?

He wished he could stay and explore the sensations and emotions knocking around inside him, but duty called. A child's life hung in the balance, and giving in to his attraction and the affection invading him wasn't an option.

He gave her a mock salute and hustled away. Glancing back once, he felt a pang of tender fondness that slowed his steps. If he wasn't careful, he'd find himself falling for her.

With determination, he broke into a jog.

Time to take down the bad guys, rescue the little damsel in distress and make it back in one piece to the woman who'd woven her way under his skin and laid siege to his heart.

A feat he thought no woman capable of.

Meghan chewed at her lip as the minutes ticked by. So far no gunfire. A good sign, she hoped.

She hated that her view of the street and the house was limited to the carport and back alley. Her foot tapped against the floorboards. Anxious energy zinged along her nerve endings, making sitting inside the stifling cruiser unbearable. She caught sight of Officer Cribs at the corner. He'd stopped to talk to a woman who'd come out of her house. No doubt telling her to go back inside where it was safe.

She should have known Ryan wouldn't feel comfortable leaving her alone. He was such a caring man underneath the gruff exterior. She hoped nothing happened to him.

Worry churned in her tummy. She cracked open the window, needing some fresh air.

A vehicle turned down the back alley and stopped beside the carport. She recognized the van. Her pulse skidded out of control. It was the same van with masked gunmen that had followed her off the freeway and had opened fire on her and Ryan. Panic seized her in a tight grip.

Two big, brawny men rushed out of the side doors each carrying an infant carrier with a squalling baby. The sound pierced her heart.

They put the babies inside a big white side-panel van, with no plates. Her blood turned to ice.

Another man left the house. He looked vaguely familiar but it was the toddler in his arms that stole her breath. Her stomach dropped. Georgina! Her wispy blond curls were matted, her pj's dirty.

They were escaping with the children.

Cribs had taken the cruiser's keys with him. She had no way of stopping the men from taking off with Georgina and the babies.

The horn!

She laid on the car horn with all her might.

The van's engine roared toward her.

Cribs ran down the sidewalk toward the cruiser.

She'd gained his attention, but unfortunately, she'd given away her presence to the bad guys in the van. The van screeched to a halt in the street beside the cruiser. The side-panel door on the van slid back and one of the men jumped out. Fear clogged her throat. The man tried the car door handle. The lock held. She drew back, thankful she'd heeded Ryan's request and stayed locked safely in the car.

Cribs drew his weapon. Through the crack in the window Meghan heard him yell, "Stop. Police."

Ignoring Cribs, her attacker pulled away his elbow then smashed it into the window. Meghan screamed and dove sideways to avoid flying glass.

The lock popped. The door opened. Terrorized, Meghan grabbed at the driver's door handle as a beefy arm snagged her around the waist and yanked her roughly out of the car. She let loose a terror-filled scream. He dragged her to the van. She kicked and yelled to no avail.

Cribs fired a shot. The sound echoed in Meghan's brain, sending her already galloping pulse into hyperdrive. Her insides felt like any second she might explode. Her attacker didn't hesitate. He threw her into the van like a sack of potatoes between the space dividing the front buckets and the middle seat bench. She landed on the floor with a thunk. Pain exploded in her hip where her cell phone dug into her flesh from inside the pocket of her capris. The man jumped in the van after her.

"Halt! Police!" Cribs cried again.

The door slid closed with a slam as the van shot forward. More gunfire. Bullets pinged off the van's back doors.

Shaking, Meghan pulled herself upright between the seats, forcing her terrified mind to take stock of the situation. There were three men in the vehicle—the driver, a man in the passenger seat and another crouched on the floor between the front captain seats.

Her frantic gaze sought Georgina. The little girl sat in the far backseat strapped in with a seat belt across her small body between two red-faced infants in tattered car seats. The babies wailed and Georgina screeched as she plucked at the buckle trying to remove the seat belt.

Meghan climbed over the bench seat to attend to the children. She squatted as best she could on the floor between the back of the bench seat and the babies.

"Shh," she cooed, trying to calm Georgina and the two crying babes. Her heart swelled with love and fear.

One of the men in the front threw a glance toward her. "Why'd we grab her?"

"Roman will be pleased. He'll take great pleasure in killing her himself," the driver replied with an evil smile. "It'll make up for failing to take her out the first time we tried."

Meghan swallowed back the wild rise of terror as horrible thoughts invaded her mind and tried to rob her of her any coherent thoughts. Despair welled up to choke her as the van continued on unimpeded. Sirens wailed in the distance. The van made lots of turns, obviously making an effort to lose themselves in the sea of New York City traffic.

She'd never see Ryan again. He would feel responsible for her capture. He was the kind of man who took ownership even when it wasn't his to take. He was such a good man, full of integrity and honor. Unlike his father.

She pushed the uncharitable thought aside. She needed to stay focused on what was happening and how to get out of this while protecting the babies.

She had to find a way to let Ryan know where she was, give him a clue how to find her. Because she trusted he'd never give up looking for her and Georgina.

The van rounded a turn. She fell on her backside. Her throbbing hip reminded her that she had her phone.

Carefully, she inched the phone out of her pocket with one hand while comforting Georgina with the other. Keeping the phone low and out of sight, she punched in 9–1–1.

She hoped it connected but couldn't dare chance bringing the phone to her ear to find out. Her only hope was to leave the line open anyway and pray for the best.

TEN

"Clear."

"Clear."

The word reverberated through the empty dwelling as several officers running point called out from various positions inside the house. The criminals had escaped out the back before the police had gotten into position.

Frustration bit a chunk out of Ryan's nerves. How was he going to tell Meghan they'd hit another dead end? Dread at how she'd take the news chewed at his gut.

A commotion at the front door drew his attention as he struggled to retrieve the phone. Cribs, looking harried and panicked, gestured as he spoke to Captain Gregson. Why wasn't the officer with Meghan?

"Where's Meghan?" Ryan demanded.

"She was taken. A silver van. Heading south," Cribs replied, his face ashen.

Terror slammed into Ryan. *Taken? A silver van?*

Images of masked gunmen, bullets flying, the blood on her arm ripped through his mind. *How?*

"Did you get the license plate number?" Ryan asked, his voice shaking.

Cribs shook his head. "No plates."

Just like the van that had chased them. It had to be the same men. Fear, stark and ugly, squeezed his lungs tight.

Meghan. Her name reverberated through his heart.

"We'll put out a BOLO, start a citywide search," Gregson said. "We'll find her."

Forcing himself to breathe, Ryan nodded. They had to find her. Digging deep within his soul, he found the edges of his faith and held on with all he was worth. *Dear Lord, please let me find her.*

"Captain!" another officer yelled. "Nine-one-one received a call. They traced the cell number. It belongs to Meghan Henry."

With hope clawing at his chest, Ryan knew they had a chance of finding her. They could use her cell phone as a GPS and, God willing, rescue her before it was too late.

The van finally stopped. A fresh wave of fear washed over Meghan. Stopping meant facing this Roman person. She shuddered. "Please, Lord, deliver me, us, from this horror," she whispered.

Through the back window Meghan saw large

metal crates stacked two or three high, creating a barrier between the road and the ocean. Commercial freighters and cargo ships lined the docks while several barges and tugboats squeezed between the large vessels, looking like toys. A shipping yard.

The three men climbed out, leaving Meghan and the children unwatched for the moment. This was her chance. Her heart beat in her throat. She bent forward and brought the phone closer. Static. The call had ended. Or maybe never connected in the first place. Praying for another chance, she pressed Redial.

The back double doors of the van jerked open. The briny scent of the ocean swirled around Meghan's head. She straightened with a start, tucking the phone between her knees.

"Hey, what are you doing?" one of the thugs yelled from the doorway.

She held up the pacifier she'd found on the floor.

The guy grunted. "Get out."

"What about the babies?" she asked, not about to leave them unattended.

"We'll get 'em," he said with impatience lacing his words.

Needing time to slip the phone back in her pocket unobserved, she purposely made a clumsy attempt at climbing over the seat. She managed to pocket the phone just as the big beefy guy who'd manhandled her earlier grabbed her by the upper arms and dragged her through the back of the van. The kids were hauled out with more care. Meghan scooped up Georgina. Immediately, her little arms went around Meghan's neck, her dimpled hands fisting in Meghan's hair. A stab of love pierced through the fear choking her.

The driver of the van grabbed her by the arm and pulled her toward a midsize cargo ship wedged in between a flat-bottomed barge and a massive freighter. The rusted metal and chipped paint showed years out on the sea. Overhead a gull cried. The brackish smells filling the air turned Meghan's stomach.

Practically jogging to keep pace with the man dragging her closer to her fate, Meghan clutched Georgina in a tight grip.

They were taken to a hold below the deck of a black-and-red cargo ship. A hard shove pushed her inside a dank room, barren except for a large cabinet in one corner. The thug stood guard at the door. A moment later the two other babies still strapped into their carriers were brought in by one of the goons. The room filled with the stench of soiled diapers.

"These children need attending to," she told the thug.

One of the men went to the cabinet and opened the doors. "Here you go."

Inside the cabinet were diapers, extra clothes, bottles, cans of formula, jugs of water and blankets. Her heart squeezed tight at the evidence that having babies aboard the vessel wasn't an unusual occurrence.

How many more children had ended up locked in this room? Who had tended to them, surely not these rough men?

The door banged shut behind the thugs, the noise echoing off the metal walls. The lock sliding into place sounded like a death knell, making Meghan shiver with dread and apprehension. Frantic, she grabbed her cell phone. Her fingers fumbled on the keys. The static beep of the phone shuddered through her. No service.

She dropped on her knees and gathered Georgina close and prayed for protection and rescue. The cry of the infants tugged at her heart. They needed her, too.

Taking care of the babies gave her something to concentrate on besides their dire predicament. The babies, one boy and one girl, couldn't have been more than six months old. Their dimpled cheeks and chubby little bodies looked well fed and cared for. Who did they belong to? Why were they in the hands of these monsters?

The questions threatened to tear down Meghan's defenses. But she would not cry or despair, not when she had these little souls depending on her.

At nearly two years old, Georgina was a big help, handing Meghan the diapers. Love for the little girl swelled in Meghan's chest. How could Christina have given her over to these awful men?

As soon as she had the babies clean and content on a blanket she'd laid out, she checked the cell again. Still no signal. She let out a frustrated growl and tucked the phone back into her pocket. It would take a miracle of God for Ryan to find her.

Thankfully, Meghan believed in miracles of God.

After a while the babies fell asleep sprawled out on the blanket. Meghan rocked a sleepy Georgina, softly singing an Irish lullaby Meghan's mother used to sing to her. Only, when her mother had sung the song, she'd had the lilting cadence of her native tongue, which made the song so much more meaningful. Meghan couldn't roll her *R*s, no matter how hard she tried, so the lullaby lost a bit of its sparkle, but it did the trick. Soon Georgina was fast asleep in Meghan's arms.

She relished this moment of peace and quiet. The fear hovered, but for the time being they were alive and safe. She wished Ryan would walk through the door. Only then would she feel secure. She'd give anything to hear his voice, to see him. To have him hold her close and tell her everything would work out.

She want him to kiss her again. She wanted to kiss him back.

Silent tears slipped from the corners of her eyes. She cared deeply for Ryan Fitzgerald. And she may never get to see him again. She sent up a gut-wrenching plea that he'd find her and she'd have a chance to tell him.

The lock on the door slid open, the noise grating in the quiet of the room. Alarm seized her heart, making the muscle stall as the door swung open. Blessedly the children slept undisturbed by the noise. Their crying had tuckered them out.

One of the thugs stepped in. Wirier with blond hair and beady eyes, he was the man she'd thought seemed familiar. Now looking at him, she flashed back to when Christina had burst through the stairwell door. This man had been with her. So much for her saying she didn't know him.

He motioned for her to come with him.

Grateful for his silence, she gently laid Georgina on the blanket between the sleeping infants. Meghan's heart pitched to think what torment the child would feel if she awoke and Meghan were gone. She didn't want to leave her little charges. "Please," she whispered. "Please let us go."

In response, the man roughly grasped her upper arm and yanked her out of the room. He then dragged her down the narrow hall. They entered what appeared to be a dining hall. Four tables with benches sat in the middle of the room. Meghan's stomach rumbled at the smell of greasy food.

Another man sat at one end of the farthest table, eating a hamburger purchased from a popular fast-food joint. He had a narrow face and dull gray eyes that studied her as if she were a tasty dessert to his dinner out of a bag. She flinched, wanting nothing more than to hide from his greasy, prob-ing gaze.

"You've cost me time and money," he said in a heavy guttural accent. "I don't like when people cost me time and money. Especially a woman."

This must be the man Mr. Sharp was so afraid of. The man Christina called Roman. He had soul-less eyes and angular features that bordered on ugly. He made a twirling motion with his index finger, which Meghan interpreted meant he wanted her to turn around.

Indignation warred with fear until she thought she might explode. She wasn't going to put on a show.

"Who are you?" she demanded, the indignation edging past the fear. If she was going to die, she was going out with a fight.

"Spirit," Roman said through a hamburger patty, special sauce… "That will be good. Fun to break." He said something else in a language she recognized as Russian. The other thug laughed, a raucous sound that sent a shiver of distaste down her spine.

"You have no right to hold me here. I demand you let me and the children go."

He shook his head. "Now why would I do that when I can make money instead?"

Meghan swallowed the panic tightening her throat. "You're making a mistake, mister. You won't get away with this," she said with more bravado than she felt.

"I already have." He rose from the table, his movements fluid, making her think of a cobra rising up ready to strike.

"There's no one to pay a ransom for me. You won't gain anything by holding me," she said, despairing the truth of her words. She had no family save Georgina left in this world. Ryan's image rose. Her heart ached for him.

"Ah, you think wrongly. There are plenty of men who will pay dearly for you. Who will like nothing better than to break that spirit you so proudly display. Even if you are older than we usually offer."

His words rammed into her with the force of a fist and a tremor of terror worked its way over her flesh.

He planned to *sell* her. And from the sound of it to more than one buyer.

Her worst nightmare had just come true.

* * *

Ryan's heart pounded in his ears. He willed Gregson to drive faster. They were headed to Brooklyn. The NYPD's Information Technology Department was using the GPS system on Meghan's cell phone to track her movements.

Gregson's dashboard radio chirped. He grabbed the mic. "Yeah."

The dispatcher's voice came across the airwaves. "The signal went dead."

Ryan's stomach dropped. No!

"Last location?" Gregson asked.

The dispatcher rattled off the address near the East River.

Ryan's eyes burned. Fear choked the breath from his lungs. Meghan. She was so special. He couldn't lose her. Clutching the door handle in a tight grip, he prayed beneath his breath.

Lord, please, let me get to her in time. If anything happens to her...

He wouldn't go there. Nor would he acknowledge the expanding emotions in his heart clamoring for his attention. They'd only known each other a short time yet it felt like a lifetime. He'd come to know her, to care about her. He wouldn't let anything happen to her.

I know I've been distant, Lord. I know I've questioned You and at times turned my back on You. Please forgive me. Please keep Meghan safe.

He focused on the surroundings. The sun hung low in the sky. Gulls cried overhead. The road they were on led to a shipping yard. Large metal containers dominated the real estate. Huge cargo ships, freighters and flat-bottomed barges laid anchor, waiting for their load. Smaller tugboats and fishing boats crowded in between the larger vessels.

Meghan was here somewhere. Inside a container? Or already aboard one of the boats?

Another horrible thought wormed its way to the forefront. Could she be at the bottom of the river?

No. He refused to believe it. She hadn't been gone that long. They weren't that far behind her. He had to find her. He would find her.

As soon as the car stopped, Ryan bolted. He didn't know where to start but he had to do something. He surveyed the area, getting a lay of the land.

"Fitzgerald, hold up," Gregson called. "Wait!"

Protocol dictated he wait. Normally, Ryan took the rules to heart. Rules, protocol, procedures all were in place for a reason. He understood that. And most days appreciated that fact. Was a stickler, actually.

But not today.

Not today when the life of the woman he cared about was on the line. All the rules, protocol and procedures went out the window with the proverbial bathwater.

He'd pay the price. He didn't care. Meghan was worth whatever happened to him.

Ignoring Gregson and the line of police cars filing in behind the captain's sedan, Ryan darted forward. His bum ankle protested. Forcing back the pain, he searched for someone, anyone he could question.

He asked a guy pushing a cart. No. Guy hadn't seen anyone matching Meghan's description.

Ryan saw a group of three dockworkers taking a smoking break, their cigarettes glowing red amid a cloud of smoke. The men all shook their heads.

Ryan wouldn't give up.

To his left, a forklift operator climbed into his rig. Ryan climbed up after him and held on to the door, trapping the guy inside the enclosed cab.

"Hey, you can't be up here," the guy said.

Ryan flashed his badge then secured it to the front loop of his belt so it would be visible. "I'm looking for a woman."

"Aren't we all," the guy retorted.

Impatience knotted Ryan's muscles. "She's blonde, about five-eight. She had on a white blouse." His voice sounded tight, constricted with the worry pressing in on him. "She may have had a toddler with her."

At mention of the toddler, the NY attitude left

the longshoreman and he nodded. "Yeah, I saw 'em. She and the kid were taken onto one of the cargo ships."

Anticipation revved Ryan's blood. "Which one? Take me there."

"Sure. Hang on." The guy started the engine then shifted the gears. The big tires rolled slowly over the asphalt. The guy pointed to a midsize rusty cargo ship that barely looked seaworthy. Deflated tires rimmed the vessel to act as bumpers against the dock. "That one. That's the one she boarded."

"Thanks." Ryan jumped down, a zing of pain shot up his leg. He gritted his teeth and ran for the cover of a container. Peering around the corner, he assessed the vessel, noting two guards on deck, one near the stern and one at the bow. Though he didn't see their weapons, he had no doubt they were carrying. He took out his cell. No bars. He had no way to communicate with NYPD. He couldn't wait for them. He needed to go now.

The bridge was empty, mostly likely the captain was belowdecks.

Ryan searched for a way on board the cargo ship.

No convenient rope hung over the starboard side; no gangway connected the vessel to the dock. In fact, the boat wasn't even moored. It looked ready to sail.

A smoke plume from the engine funnel gave testament to his thought. Meghan. He had to get on board.

His gaze snagged on the larger freight vessel to the aft of the barge. A gangplank was being used to load freight on board.

In a low crouch, he ran for the large vessel and raced up the gangway, eliciting curious glances from the longshoremen securing crates of melons on board. He crouched behind the railing. With caution, he peered over the side to the boat below.

A ten-foot drop. Maybe fifteen.

No big deal. He'd jumped out of a sugar maple tree much taller when he was twelve. The landing had been jarring but he'd walked away on his own two feet. He flexed his still-tender ankle and breathed in deep, feeling a slight pinch in his ribs. Okay, maybe jumping wouldn't be the best idea, but it was the only one he had.

His gaze tripped over the cargo deck below his position.

Wait, a rope ladder hung on the port side away from the dock and dangled in the water.

His way on board.

"Thank You, God. I appreciate it," he murmured.

From the deck of the freighter he could see NYPD spreading out, doing a grid search. He needed to alert them without alerting the bad guys.

A longshoreman stepped onto the freighter's deck. Ryan showed his badge and pointed to the officers on the dock. "See those cops?"

The guy nodded.

"I need you to get a message to them. Them tell she's on the black-and-red cargo ship."

"She's on the cargo ship," the guy repeated.

Ryan nodded. "Go. Hurry."

The guy quickly made his way off the freighter.

Ryan followed and then slipped into the murky water from the dock. The smell of gasoline and brine filled his head as he cut a path through the lapping waves, every stroke of his arms causing pain in his ribs but nothing he couldn't handle.

He was careful to keep close to the vessel so he wouldn't be seen from the cargo ship where they were keeping Meghan. He reached the rope ladder and hauled himself on board.

Water dripped from his clothing. A chill ran down his spine. He smelled like the East River or worse, the NY sewage system.

A guard patrolled the deck. The man, bald, thick-necked and barrels for biceps carried an AK-47. Heavy firepower. Ryan let out a controlled breath to calm his careening pulse. He ducked behind a group of rusted steel drums without detection.

He held his breath as the guard continued past his hiding spot. He considered his options—wait until the guard came back by and take him out, or risk making a run for the door that led belowdecks.

The longer he remained undetected, the safer Meghan and Georgina would be because NYPD would be swarming the boat any second. The sooner he got to Meghan before the bad guys realized the authorities were on to them, the better. That left one option. He risked making a run for the door.

He slipped inside unnoticed. His heart pounded in his chest. Adrenaline pumped through his veins. Cautiously he searched for Meghan. The trail of water he left in his wake couldn't be helped. He prayed no one noticed.

Men's voices alerted Ryan of the approaching enemy. He evaded detection by slipping inside an empty room, which looked to be the galley. He crossed to another door, which led to the mess hall. Empty, as well. He found another door and went through to another corridor. He tried to get his bearings but decided it didn't matter. He kept searching.

The faint wail of a baby kick-started a fresh wave of adrenaline. Sure the noise would lead him to Meghan, he raced to the sound and skidded to a halt outside an open door. A single overhead bulb cast shadows around the windowless room.

Ryan's heart stalled in his chest. Fear pressed down on him as he took in the scene.

Meghan stood between a nasty goon and three innocent children, two infants lying on a blanket and Georgina sitting between them with tears running down her face.

The fierceness on Meghan's beautiful face took Ryan's breath away. She was strong and courageous and determined. His heart cried out for her.

The thug chanted at Meghan in a foreign language before snarling in English, "Give me the kid."

Holding up a hand to ward off an attack, she shouted, "No. You are not taking her."

She was protecting the children against a lowlife who would clearly do her harm. Pride for her swelled inside Ryan even as rage balled his fists.

"Move!" The goon lurched for Meghan. She danced back, nearly tripping over a baby seat.

Taking advantage of her momentary imbalance, the thug grabbed her and wrapped his beefy fingers around her slender throat. She clawed at him like a wildcat.

Crazed by the sight of Meghan being hurt, Ryan lunged for the guy with a guttural growl. He knocked him sideways. Ryan smashed his fist into the guy's face. Twice.

"Ryan! Enough. Stop." Meghan's plea infiltrated his mind. "You have to stop."

Her words drew him out of his rage. He abruptly halted midswing and realized the man wasn't fighting back. Self-reproach and shame washed over him. He quickly checked the thug's pulse. Faint, but there. The guy was unconscious. He'd live.

Ryan pushed painfully to his feet. His sore ribs throbbed. Guilt for losing his control swamped him. He'd been so enraged over what had happened to Meghan he could have killed the perp with his bare hands.

He gathered Meghan close. "Are you okay?" he asked, knowing she wasn't, not really. How could she be?

She'd been shot at, kidnapped, assaulted. But she was in his arms and for the moment that was all that mattered to him.

She wrapped her arms around his middle and hung on tight. "I prayed you'd find me."

"I prayed I would, too," he said, his voice husky with fear and joy all bundled up into one strong emotion that seared him to his soul and scared him spitless. "God answered both of our prayers."

He wanted to kiss her, but time was of the essence. They had to move. Now.

With one arm he scooped up the little girl and deposited her into Meghan's arms. "We're not safe yet."

After securing the two babies in their carriers, he hefted one in each hand. "Follow me," he instructed, hoping he could get them off the boat in one piece.

ELEVEN

Meghan ran after Ryan with Georgina on her hip. She still couldn't believe he'd found her. God had come through for her. The whole moment was imbedded in her brain, burning in its intensity. One minute she thought her life was ending at the hands of a monster and then Ryan appeared.

She'd never been so happy to see anyone in her whole life. It was more than gratefulness at being rescued that made her heart pound. And made her mouth go dry with a fear far different than that of a physical threat. But now was not the time to process what she felt. They had to get the little ones off the barge and to safety.

Ryan led the way through the dining room and kitchen. He halted as shouts echoed down the outside corridor.

Her guard had been found.

She sent up another plea to Heaven. *Lord, You brought us this far. Just a little farther, please.*

"There's a door that leads to the deck at the end of this hall. When we get out, head to the left side of the deck and hide behind a stack of steel drums," Ryan instructed.

Holding Georgina tighter, she nodded, prepared to do whatever necessary to protect the children.

"On three," he said.

"On three."

He leaned close and placed a quick kiss on her lips. Stunned, she took reassurance in the intimate gesture. He would lead them to safety. She trusted him to.

They made it down the short hall to the deck. The minute they emerged, an armed man shouted a warning before pointing a large caliber rifle in their direction. The loud retort of a bullet leaving the muzzles startled Meghan.

Thwack. A bullet slammed into the wood beside Ryan's head.

"Go!" Ryan urged. "The barrels."

Protecting Georgina with her body from the spray of bullets pinging off the deck, Meghan flew to the safety found behind the steel drums. Ryan made it behind her. He tucked the carriers with two screaming babies into a nook between two drums. He withdrew his weapon and fired back. The loud noise made Georgina screech. Meghan covered the little girl's ears with her hands even as her own ears rang from the gun's close proximity.

More gunfire exploded.

"Halt! Police!"

"Drop your weapons!"

Relief rushed the breath from Meghan's lungs. A deathly silence descended.

A man's shout rang out. "Ryan Fitzgerald!"

"Here," Ryan said and slowly stood.

Meghan followed suit. Her eyes widened. Uniformed law enforcement officers surrounded the bad guys left standing. Several were on the deck, dead or wounded, she didn't know.

"We need help with the kids," Ryan called out.

Officers rushed forward and carried the babies off the ship. Meghan wouldn't release Georgina as she walked off the ship, careful to shield Georgina's eyes from seeing the trail of bodies strewn across the deck. She averted her own eyes.

An officer escorted her to a parked cruiser. "It'll be a little while before we get moving," the officer informed her before walking away.

Meghan sank into the backseat and snuggled Georgina close. "We're safe, little one. We made it," she murmured. Ryan had promised they'd find Georgina and they had. He was an amazing man. Her heart filled with joy and tenderness.

A few minutes later Ryan joined her in the backseat. "We made it," he said.

His words echoed her own thoughts. "Yes. Thanks to you," she replied, entwining her fingers through his. The intimacy of the car wrapped around her. "Where are the babies?"

"Safe in another car with two officers watching over them until CPS can get here."

Glad to hear the babies were safe, she searched his face and asked, "How did you find me?"

"Your phone has GPS," he explained. "That was smart thinking on your part."

"I was afraid the call hadn't gone through."

"It did. And we were able to follow the signal to the docks."

"Where you rescued me." She squeezed his hand. "My hero."

He lifted her hand to his lips and gently kissed each knuckle. "You weren't exactly a simpering princess waiting to be rescued."

"I didn't stand a chance, though. Those men were going to sell Georgina and the babies." Her voice shook as she added, "And me. If they didn't kill me first."

Ryan's expression darkened. "When that goon had his hands wrapped around your throat…I went a little crazy."

"You did." She shuddered as the moment replayed itself in her mind. "It was a little scary."

"I'm sorry. I shouldn't have lost control like that. I can't stand to see anyone, especially a woman, abused."

"I would imagine you see it a lot in your line of work," she said.

"Not that much in Fitzgerald Bay, thankfully. But in college—" He broke off, his lips pressing together.

"In college?" she prompted. "What happened while you were in college?"

His expression darkened, his gaze taking on a faraway glaze. "I witnessed my best friend beat up his girlfriend."

She winced with empathy. "Was she okay?"

"In time," he said. "I stopped him, but not before he'd busted a few of her facial bones."

Meghan cringed, knowing the pain firsthand. "That's painful."

"Yeah, she had to have reconstructive surgery." He shook his head. "But she wouldn't press charges. So I did."

"You did?" She stared at this man. How could she have ever doubted him? His sense of justice, of right and wrong, defined him, made him the man he was. A man full of integrity and honor.

A man worth loving.

She swallowed hard on that last thought. She'd never thought she'd find a man like him. Wasn't sure they even existed. Maybe in fairy tales. But not in real life. Not her life.

He nodded. "I sent my best friend to jail because she wouldn't."

This she understood, too. "She was too afraid he'd do worse the next time if she filed a complaint."

Ryan searched her face. "You're right, she was afraid. How did you know that?"

Averting her gaze, she watched Georgina play with the buttons on her blouse. Her pulse kicked up as she confessed, "Because that was what kept me from reporting my husband."

When he didn't respond, she glanced up to see stunned anger on his face.

"Your husband beat you?"

"My ex-husband," she said with emphasis. "I finally found the courage to divorce him."

"I knew you'd been married and divorced, but I had no idea…"

She frowned at the self-recrimination in his tone. He took so much responsibility onto himself. Responsibilities that weren't his to bear. It didn't surprise her in the least that he'd run a background check on her. He was thorough that way. "There were no police reports filed, so how could you have known? And what would knowing have changed?"

He blinked. "I don't know." His expression

turned puzzled. "You're so brave and strong willed, I can't imagine you letting anyone take advantage of you."

She shrugged. "I was young and weak then." She wasn't that person anymore. "But the pain and suffering toughened me up. That and a nurse named Justine. She helped me get to a shelter. Helped me find my way back to God."

"Praise God for that," he said, his gaze soft and tender.

"Yes. Praise God." Affection for this wonderful man made her smile. "I've never had someone fight for me before."

"I'll always fight for you," he said quietly.

Her heart jumped. She wanted to believe him. But she'd had promises made to her before. Promises that were broken in the worst possible way. "I hope there's never a need for that again."

Ryan slipped an arm around her and drew her to his side. "You're safe now." He chucked a wide-eyed Georgina under the chin. "So are you, little one."

Georgina ducked her head and buried her face in Meghan's shoulder. Meghan gently patted her back in a soothing rhythm as yearning and care filled her.

"Did they capture Roman?" she asked with a shiver of dread, thinking about the soulless man who'd made it clear she'd earned his wrath.

"No. Unfortunately, the leader, Roman Wykoski, escaped. He's wanted by the FBI as well as Interpol." Ryan tightened his hold on her.

"He was very angry that I'd messed up his plans." The threat of his wrath hung over her like a dark cloud.

Ryan frowned. "Don't worry. He'll be captured. He won't bother you ever again."

She wanted to believe that but a tight knot of apprehension formed in her chest. She wouldn't truly feel safe until the man was caught. Thankful for Ryan's steady presence, she leaned her head on Ryan's shoulder. She even didn't mind his damp shirt or odor from his swim in the river. She was glad he was there.

She didn't know what the future held, but for this moment, she would take the comfort he offered.

"Meghan, honey," Ryan's voice held a new note of tension.

She sat up abruptly, fear jolting through her system. "What is it?"

He nodded toward another sedan that had roared to a halt a few feet away. "Child Protective Services."

Frowning she watched a man and women emerge from the car. Panic twisted in her stomach. She turned to face Ryan. "Please, don't let them take Georgina from me."

The sad and resigned expression on his face didn't bode well. "They have to. It's protocol. I've broken enough rules today that I won't have any sway."

"But Olivia wanted me to have Georgina," she insisted. "Christina's in jail. Georgina has no one else."

"I'm sure the authorities will take Olivia's wish into account as well as Christina's role in the human trafficking." He glanced away, his jaw tightening.

She knew what he was thinking—making Olivia's revealing letter public would hurt his father and his reputation. Empathy twisted in her chest, but she forced it down. His father had lied and covered up his part in her cousin's death. Christina Hennessy had bought Georgina illegally and now sat in jail, accused of killing her husband and suspected of killing Olivia. Meghan was Georgina's last living relative.

The only way she stood a chance at gaining custody of Georgina was to reveal the truth in a court of law.

She would do what she had to do. No matter the price she would pay.

"They're coming," Ryan said.

She made a distressed sound and hugged Georgina to her chest.

"You have to do what's best for Georgina," he stated gently, "and right now it's going with CPS. They will care for her until we can get her back."

We. She hoped he meant that.

Meghan's eyes filled with tears. "I want to adopt her. And the other babies if their parents can't be found." They needed her. She needed them. She'd always wanted a family of her own. When she'd been married she'd longed to have a child, but her ex had refused. Then after the divorce she'd resigned herself to a lonely, solitary existence. But now she had a chance to be a mother.

She stared into Ryan's blue eyes. He brushed a lock of hair away from her face. "You'll make a great mom. I'm sure a judge will see that."

His praise sent pleasure gliding through her. If only he thought she'd make a good wife…but she didn't even know how he felt about her. And after her article hit the front page… She didn't want to even think about that yet.

The car door opened and a man leaned down. "Deputy Chief, I'm Alan Lancore with CPS. We need to take the child into custody."

Meghan tightened her hold on Georgina. "Can we have just another few moments?"

Lancore nodded. He gestured toward the sedan he'd arrived in. "I'll be waiting over there."

Meghan showered kisses on Georgina, causing

the little girl to giggle with glee. "You're going to be okay, sweetie," she said. "I'll do everything in my power to make sure we're together."

Even if that meant destroying the reputation of Aiden Fitzgerald.

And costing her the chance of having Ryan in her life.

But what choice did she have?

By the time they'd returned to Fitzgerald Bay, the moon had risen and cast silvery shadows over the dunes, creating a picturesque scene of light and dark that Meghan never tired of seeing.

Ryan walked Meghan to the door of her cottage. The quaint little beach house, with its white picket fence and beautiful stonework, sat back off the beach sheltered by gently rolling sand dunes.

The rumble of the ocean waves crashing on the shore echoed the thunderous beating of her heart. Mist blowing in from the water dampened her hair, making her shiver.

"Cold?" Ryan asked, rubbing her arms.

Cold, overwrought and heartsick at having to be away from Georgina. "I miss her already," she whispered, tears clogging her throat.

He pulled her close. They'd both showered and changed after their ordeal, using the NYPD's locker rooms. She wore a borrowed tracksuit from a female officer. He wore sweats, a fresh T-shirt and a pair of flip-flops, replacing his ruined shoes. The faint scent of soap clung to his skin. She wrapped her arms around him, aware of every point of contact. She tilted her head back. Their gazes locked.

He dipped his head and captured her lips, in a kiss filled with pent-up fear, hope and words that needed to be said. She reveled in the sensations coursing through her, in the emotions rising to the surface. She never wanted the kiss to end. When he eased away his mouth, she nearly cried out at the loss of contact.

Breathing hard, he touched his forehead to hers. "Wow."

She smiled. "Yeah. Wow."

For a long moment they remained still and quiet. Hoping they could talk and figure out what was going on between them, she asked softly, "Would you like to come in? I could make us some tea."

He drew back but kept his arms snuggly around her. Shadows played across his features, hiding his thoughts. "I need to write up my report. I'm sure the chief will have questions."

The chief of police. His father. The subject of the article she planned to write. Unease slithered down her spine. As much as she hoped the piece would not only bring justice to her cousin's memory and advance her career, she didn't want to hurt Ryan.

"Can't you do that in the morning?" she asked, hoping to stave off reality for a bit longer. She didn't want to think about how her article would affect him or his feelings for her.

"I could," he admitted softly. But she heard the *but* in his voice. "We're both wiped out and need some rest. Some time to think coherently."

Her heart pinched at his words. He was right of course. There was no denying the physical attraction was strong between them. But the emotional attachment, the expanding feelings sprouting roots in her heart, made moving in any direction treacherous.

She had no idea how he felt. Maybe this was his way of letting her know he wasn't interested in pursuing a relationship with her. The thought depressed her nearly as much as being away from Georgina did.

"You'll keep me apprised of the case?" she asked, not willing to break their bond yet.

"I will," he promised, seeming in no hurry to let go his hold on her.

"Monday I'll be hiring an attorney to fight for custody of Georgina," she told him. "He may need to talk to you."

"Not a problem. I'll help you in any way I can."

A question rose to the forefront of her mind.

Her mouth went dry with a fresh kind of fear. "Do you think your family will petition for custody of Georgina?"

His silence battered at her, upping her anxiety tenfold.

Finally, he spoke, his voice low and careful. "I can't give you a definitive answer until I speak with my dad. I know we'd like to keep this situation 'in-house' so to speak."

Meaning out of the public purview. Apprehension crunched through her tummy. She had to make him understand that wouldn't be possible. As a journalist she had an obligation to write the truth. And that truth would be instrumental in her custody case. She doubted very much that the court wouldn't want to know the full extent of Georgina's heritage. "Ryan—"

"Shh." He pressed his finger to her lips. A part of her wished it could have been his lips touching hers. "Tomorrow will be soon enough to discuss all this. I'm sure my father will want to have a meeting. I'll talk to him. Then we'll go from there."

"But you need to know—"

His mouth captured hers once again, cutting off her words. She lifted her arms around his neck and kissed him back, giving in to the bundle of emotions bouncing around her head and heart. When they parted, she was breathless and a little light-headed. All thoughts of a story left her.

"My brother Charles and Demi are celebrating their engagement tomorrow night," he said softly, almost hesitantly. "I was hoping you'd come with me." He swallowed as if finding his words difficult. "As my date."

Thrilled by the invitation and the way he was looking at her with such vulnerable expectation, as if he wasn't sure she'd agree, she smiled wide and nodded. "Of course I'll go with you. As your date."

No shadows could hide the pleased expression on his handsome face. She marveled that she'd ever thought him cold. He wore his emotions right out in the open for the world to see. For her to see. The words *I love you* hovered on the tip of her tongue. And realization knocked the breath from her lungs.

But fear of taking that most important step kept her silent.

They'd been through so much together. Shared their hurts and the triumph of rescuing Georgina. Meghan had to be cautious and not jump into anything too quickly. Every decision she made now would affect her bid to gain custody of Georgina. She had to be smart and take things slowly. With a sigh, she slid her arms from around his neck and placed her palms on his chest over his heart. "What's the dress code for tomorrow?"

"Casual. The celebration will be at Aunt Vanessa's."

Vanessa Connolly, Aiden's sister, ran Connolly's Catch seafood restaurant with her fisherman husband, Joe Connolly. Meghan had dined there often this past winter for their clam chowder. The best she'd ever had on many a cold blustery day. "Are you sure she won't mind having me join you last-minute like this?"

He gave a soft laugh. "No. She won't mind. She took over the role of hostess for the Fitzgerald family celebrations after Mom died. Aunt Vanessa loves to throw a party and the more guests the better."

"What about the rest of your family?" She tugged on her bottom lip with her teeth. "I wouldn't want to intrude on their celebration."

He kissed the tip of her nose. "Don't worry. You'll be with me."

She liked the sound of that.

"Your keys?" he asked.

She handed them over.

"I don't like the idea of you being alone here," he said. "I'll have a patrol come by hourly until Roman is caught."

Dread rose to rob her of the peace she'd been feeling. "Thank you."

He opened the door, walked inside and flipped on the lights. The warm glow played across his handsome face as he drew her into his arms once again, tucking her head beneath his chin. She clung to him. After several heartbeats, he let her go. "Call me if you get scared or need anything. I'm just down the beach. I could be here within minutes."

His offer warmed her heart. "I will. I promise."

"Good night. I'll see you tomorrow."

She closed the door behind him.

The click of the lock would keep her safe from the lingering threat of Roman's retribution, but keep Ryan out, too. For now.

She released a wistful sigh. She missed him already. Missed his strength, missed his smile, missed him.

A piece of her heart walked away with him. And she wanted it back. Wanted him back.

Just as she wanted Georgina back in her arms.

Tomorrow. The word held such promise.

Maybe one day soon, she'd have both Ryan and Georgina permanently in her life.

TWELVE

Ryan slept late on Saturday morning and then headed to his office around noon. He'd kept his phone beside him all night in case Meghan had needed him. She hadn't called. The patrol reported all was quiet at her house. There was a mountain of paperwork he had to take care of before he could enjoy the evening with Meghan. And his family. A much different event than the last time he'd brought her into their midst.

A nervous quiver shot through him.

He'd never felt this way about another woman. It scared him and thrilled at the same time.

A stack of reports and forms full of questions related to the events of the past few days waited on his desk, claiming the next few hours of his concentration. An official reprimand initiated by Captain Gregson for recklessly endangering Ryan's own life had been added to his employee work file.

His father was beyond angry with him. The reaming he'd received last night from his dad when he'd checked in had given Ryan a headache. But hadn't fazed Ryan nearly as deeply as it once would have since he was upset still with his father.

Ryan had a lot of work to do on the whole forgiveness concept. He was trying, really he was. But every time he thought about how his father's actions had been the catalyst for the past week's event, he'd get choked with anger.

"The DNA results are back." Douglas interrupted Ryan's concentration from the doorway of the office, holding what must be the report in his hands.

Anticipation kick-started Ryan's pulse. "Finally. Was it Christina Hennessy's blood on the rock?"

Douglas walked closer and consulted the paper. "Yes."

Ryan let out a cynical laugh. "Why am I not surprised? She claims Burke did the deed."

"Then how would her blood get on the stone?" Douglas countered.

"Good question." One he wanted answered by the potential liar herself.

He ran a hand over his jaw. The bristles of a five-o'clock shadow scraped along his palm. He was tired. Tired of this investigation, tired of the unanswered questions and tired of feeling like he was failing Meghan Henry. Despite motive and her DNA on the murder weapon, they still didn't have enough evidence to convict Christina for

Meghan's cousin's murder. That bothered him. She wouldn't have closure until the murder was solved.

"You up for a little road trip?" Ryan asked.

Douglas arched a black eyebrow. "To visit Christina in Rikers?"

"Actually Framingham. She's being transferred to MCI Monday or Tuesday." The Massachusetts Correctional Institute for women was located north of Boston. Christina would be held there pending her arraignment and trial. "Maybe we'll catch a break, and she'll confess."

"You're on. Just let me know the time and day." Douglas checked his watch. "I'd better get going. Merry said she had something important to tell me before we head to the party." His blue eyes twinkled. "I'll see you and your date tonight."

Ryan couldn't stop the lopsided grin on his face. "Yes. You will."

He had a date with Meghan Henry. He'd never counted on that. Hadn't ever thought he'd find someone he would willingly bring into the family fold. But he had. Meghan was so much more than he'd first imagined. She was light and dark and every color in between. She painted his world with joy and hope.

He shoved away from the desk. There was no sense in trying to work. Not when all he could think about was Meghan and the upcoming evening. It wouldn't be a romantic night, not with the whole Fitzgerald clan in attendance. But it would be a beginning.

In the hallway, he ran into his youngest brother, Owen. Hurt weaseled its way to the surface. He tried to ignore it. "Hey."

"Hey, heard you've had a busy few days," Owen said, his brown eyes twinkling in his normal good-natured way.

Love for his sibling warred with the sense of betrayal Ryan felt. Owen and Charles had kept the secret of Olivia's parentage from him. This was the first time a secret had come between them. "Yeah. Busy."

Ryan tried to slip past him.

Owen grabbed his arm. He stopped to stare at his brother.

"We hated keeping the secret from you," Owen said. "From everyone."

The contrition on Owen's face made Ryan say, "Then why did you?"

Owen dropped his hand. "Dad asked us to," he stated simply.

Ryan wanted to be angry with Owen for choosing his loyalty to their father over his loyalty to him. But when push came to shove, Ryan knew their father had put his brothers in a difficult position. "I don't like secrets."

Owen nodded. "I know, bro. I'm sorry we kept one from you. Truly. Can you forgive me?"

Ryan's heart softened, the hurt soothed. Why was forgiving his baby brother so much easier than his father?

"I can still take you down any day of the week," Ryan quipped, referring to the wrestling matches they frequently engaged in, especially when they were kids and Owen had wanted to prove he was as strong and big as his older brothers.

"Just you try," Owen dared back. "This Sunday."

The family gathered every Sunday at the Aiden Fitzgerald home for dinner. It was a time of connecting and eating and playing. Wrestling, too.

"You're on." Ryan clapped him on the back. "You'll be at the party tonight, right?"

"Yep. I'll be bringing Victoria and Paige."

"When are you and Victoria going to set a date?" They'd been engaged for a few months now. Ryan didn't understand why they were waiting. He narrowed his gaze on his brother. "You getting cold feet?"

"No way," Owen said. "We'll get to it."

"Make it soon, brother. Victoria and Paige have waited long enough to become officially part of the Fitzgerald family."

Owen's eyebrows rose. "I didn't realize you were such an advocate for marriage." A wicked gleam entered his light blue eyes. "You meet someone recently?"

"Not recently, no." About six months ago. The day Meghan Henry walked into his life.

"Ah. So the rumors are true?"

Ryan frowned. He disliked gossip almost as much as he did secrets. "What rumors?"

"You and Meghan Henry getting chummy. Having dinner dates and running all over the place together like a couple of superheroes, saving children and…who knows what else."

His brother winked.

Ryan's mouth worked to deny the accusation but nothing came out. Yes, they had become "chummy" for lack of a better phrase. He felt a connection to her he'd never felt with anyone else. "I'm bringing her tonight."

Owen's eyebrows shot up. "That's big. Huge."

A little annoyed by his brother's overreaction, Ryan held up a hand. "I'm telling you now so you don't make a scene when we arrive."

"Scene? When who arrives?" Keira Fitzgerald asked as she joined her brothers in the hallway. Her dark straight hair was pulled back in her customary low ponytail. Her uniform was crisp and clean.

"When he arrives tonight with Meghan Henry," Owen said with relish.

Keira's eyes widened. "You're bringing her to Charles and Demi's engagement party?"

Better to get the razzing over with, Ryan thought. "Yes. I am. You have a problem with that?"

A wicked grin broke over her face. "Naw. No problem. Wow, Mr. Commitment-shy is bringing a date to meet the family. What about Sunday dinner?"

"Maybe." He hadn't thought that far ahead yet. But the thought bounced around his head. "I'm not sure."

Keira chuckled. "I think you should. She's one gutsy woman."

Pride infused Ryan. "Yes, she is. She went through a lot this past week and held up admirably. Now Christina's in jail, and little Georgina's safe."

"I'm glad you found Christina. I was tired of answering the tip lines. There sure are some wackos out there," she said.

A tight fist of apprehension lodged in Ryan's gut. "What do you mean, wackos?"

"You know, the ones who call to say aliens abducted her or that she's with Elvis in Graceland."

Regular wackos. There was still one very mean and dangerous threat out there. Ryan would feel a lot better once they caught Roman Wykoski. Having him roaming around on the loose made

Ryan edgy. He wouldn't rest until Wykoski was captured. He'd probably already fled the country; crawling back to whatever hidey-hole he'd come from.

At least Ryan could be confident the man wouldn't come anywhere near Fitzgerald Bay.

Or Meghan.

Meghan hoped the jean skirt, ruffled blouse and strappy sandals weren't too fancy or too casual for an engagement party. She was hoping for just right. She'd changed clothes at least three times, nervous over spending time with Ryan's family in such a social setting.

Footsteps sounded on the porch. She smoothed her hair and checked her lipstick in the mirror hanging on the wall beside the front door. Her flushed cheeks had nothing to do with the temperature and everything to do with the man who would be her date tonight.

Taking a deep breath, she opened the door.

Her heart did a little skip of joy at the sight of Ryan. He wore cargo pants, a T-shirt that stretched over his muscled chest and hugged his biceps attractively, and loafers. His grin made her tummy do a cartwheel.

"Hi," she said and stepped onto the porch to close the door behind her.

"Hi, yourself. You look great."

Pleased by his compliment, she smiled. "You, too."

Since the marina, where the party was being held, wasn't that far they walked. "How's the ankle?" she asked, noticing he wasn't limping.

"Good as new."

"Amazing, considering the abuse you took this week," she said, fighting back a shudder at the memories threatening to ruin this beautiful evening.

"What can I say? I'm a fast healer." He tucked her hand in the crook of his arm.

She relished the connectedness of the gesture.

The sound of the waves crashing on shore swirled around them as they headed toward the marina. An unnerving sensation slithered into her awareness. The feeling of being watched—followed—gripped her. She glanced behind them. There was no one there.

"You okay?" Ryan asked.

Dismissing the feeling, she laughed. "Yes. Just a bit spooked still."

"Understandable." He pulled her closer. "Did you catch the score for the Red Sox game today?"

Forcing herself to relax and focus, she shook her head. "I didn't. I slept most of the day," she confessed. "Who were they playing? And more importantly, did they win?"

"I don't know." He laughed. "I was hoping you'd know. I slept half the day and worked the other half."

"We're a pair, aren't we?" she said.

"Yes. We are," he agreed with a smile.

The conversation turned to books and movies as they made their way to the restaurant, discovering they shared similar tastes in both. But the whole while, she couldn't shake the sensation that someone was watching them.

Ten minutes later they climbed the wooden steps to the front door of Connolly's Catch restaurant. Lively music came from inside. Meghan drew in a nervous breath.

"It'll be great," Ryan assured her as they stepped inside. She glanced one more time behind her. Shifting shadows beyond the glare of the restaurant lights made her uneasy. Then the door closed, blocking out the night and the threats it hid.

The delicious aromas of spices and sauces tantalized her senses. As did the tacky nautical decor of the restaurant. Somehow the decorations worked, though, making the place entertaining rather than gaudy. Nets draped in the corners were dotted with blue-and-green antique glass sails. Crossed harpoons draped the walls below paintings of whalers in longboats and seaside landscapes. The jawbone of a whale, jerry-rigged with well-seasoned corded ropes, hung suspended above the dining area. The tabletops and wooden benches were reminiscent of the worn plank decks of sailing ships from days gone by.

Ryan led Meghan through the main dining hall, waving to various patrons on the way to a private room in the back. Decorated much like the center room, a glass roof gave not only a more open feel to the space but also a spectacular view of the twinkling night sky overhead. In the multiple windows in the room, moonlight captured the white caps of waves as the ocean lapped at the shore of the bay.

The room quieted as they entered. Meghan fought the urge to hide behind Ryan's broad back. His wide shoulders were strong, and she needed every bit of strength they could provide. But no sense cowering. Instead, she lifted her chin and smiled. She'd been invited to this family gathering, rightfully so this time.

A middle-age, brown-haired woman with an infectious grin, blue eyes and a smattering of freckles weaved her way through the group. She stopped in front of Meghan and Ryan. "Well, it's about time Ryan brought a date."

Meghan's cheeks flamed. She'd met Vanessa Connolly months ago, back before she'd known the Connollys and Fitzgeralds were related. She liked the older woman.

"Aunt Vanessa, this is Meghan," Ryan said.

"I know who she is. The whole family's abuzz about it."

Beside her Ryan groaned. She looked at him. His cheeks had turned red, too. She grinned. He arched an eyebrow.

Meghan turned back to Vanessa. "Thank you for having me."

"We are so glad you came." Vanessa drew her away from Ryan. "Come have something to eat and mingle."

Meghan threw a glance over her shoulder at Ryan. He winked. She winked back and was delighted by the surprise widening his eyes.

"You know my brother Aiden, but have you met our other brother, Mickey? He's the fire chief." Vanessa stopped in front of a tall man with salt-and-pepper hair, blue eyes and a trim beard.

Over the next hour, Meghan met four generations of Connollys and Fitzgeralds. Firefighters and cops dominated the professions of the adults. Kids of all sizes and ages ran around the room, laughing and giggling. A little overwhelmed, Meghan let her gaze wander toward Ryan. He sat at a wooden table, arm wrestling with a younger man with the same black hair and blue eyes as the rest of the Fitzgerald clan. Meghan thought she remembered his name as Jamie Fitzgerald, one of Mickey's sons.

Ryan lifted his eyes. Their gazes locked. A silent bond arced between them that excluded anyone else. She felt special, cared for. He grinned. Her breath caught. He held her gaze and pinned his opponent's arm to the table. Meghan laughed, amused by his he-man display, and clapped. He was so handsome and strong…and her date tonight. A sigh of pleasure welled up inside her. She hoped to have many more dates with him.

A commotion at the door drew everyone's attention and sent a jolt of fear through Meghan.

"You gotta tell me what happened to my father," a tall blond young man said, trying to push his way into the room.

Meghan let out a breath and worked to calm her racing heart. Douglas and Owen boxed him in. "This is a private party, Hennessy."

Across the room, Ryan rose to join his brothers. The three of them hustled the younger man out the door.

A stab of sympathy hit Meghan.

"Who was that?" Demi asked at Meghan's side.

"Burke Hennessy's son, Cooper, from his first marriage," Meghan replied. "He was in love with Olivia."

"Oh, that poor young man."

Meghan agreed. He'd lost the woman he loved and his father within the last six months. It would be a lot of trauma for anyone to take.

Thinking of traumas, Meghan turned to Demi.

"I owe you an apology for trying to warn you off Charles."

Compassion lit her green eyes. "You were concerned for my safety. I can appreciate that, even if you and the rest of the town were wrong about him."

"I'm glad he's no longer a suspect." Meghan glanced at the beautiful ring gracing Demi's finger. Longing caught her off guard. She touched her own barren ring finger. She wanted to marry again, maybe even a Fitzgerald. Ryan Fitzgerald. *Whoa, don't get ahead of yourself,* she thought. Aloud, she said, "I know you two will be very happy together."

"We will be," Demi agreed with a big smile. She pulled Meghan into a quick hug. "I'm so glad you came."

Tears sprang to Meghan's eyes at the display of welcome and friendship. "Me, too."

Ryan returned to the room, his expression troubled. Meghan excused herself from Demi and went to him. "Everything okay?"

He ran a hand through his dark hair. "Yeah, I think so. Cooper's pretty distraught. He was asking about his little sister. Wanting to know that Georgina was okay."

"Did you tell him Georgina was Olivia's child?"

He shook his head. "Didn't seem the right place and time."

She studied him. "Something's bothering you."

"Cooper said something about Christina's family being all insane."

"I was under the impression that besides Dosha, Christina didn't have any other family."

"Exactly."

Meghan's reporter antennae went up. What did Cooper mean?

The dinging of metal against glass drew their attention. Aiden tapped a spoon against his water glass.

Ryan snaked an arm around Meghan and leaned in close. "Let's not think about Christina or any of that tonight."

She melted against him, loving the feel of possession and protection wrapping around her, the sense of belonging. Something she'd craved for a very long time. "Sounds like a good idea," she whispered back.

"I'd like to make a toast," Aiden said.

Everyone scrambled to grab his or her drinks. Ryan snagged two glasses of lemonade and handed one to Meghan.

"To Charles and Demi," Aiden said. "May the Lord smile upon you, joy and peace be faithful companions, love wash away all sorrow and long life be yours so that you may see your children's children."

Glasses were raised, and a chorus of voices filled the room. *"Sláinte!"*

Meghan lifted her glass and repeated the Irish word for cheers. Then she clinked her glass with Ryan before sipping the tart drink.

Charles raised his hand until the room was relatively quiet again. "Thank you all for joining us in celebrating our engagement."

"When's the big day?" someone shouted.

Demi whispered something into Charles's ear. He smiled, nodded, then turned to the crowd. "Soon."

Claps and cheers went up.

Ryan leaned over. "A Fitzgerald wedding is a big deal."

"I can imagine," she said and hoped she'd be attending with Ryan. She wondered what being a bride and planning a wedding with so much family would be like. A Fitzgerald wedding would be in the beautiful sanctuary of the Fitzgerald Bay Community Church with the whole town in attendance.

"But this night isn't just about us," Charles said. "Douglas and Merry have something they'd like to share."

Ryan snickered. "I bet I can guess."

Curiosity piqued, she slanted him a glance. "Oh?"

He mouthed the word *baby* just as Douglas spoke.

"Merry and I are expecting."

More cheers and clapping engulfed the party. A new child would be welcomed and loved by all of these people. Georgina would be welcomed and loved, as well. Maybe one day Meghan and Georgina could be a part of this family.

"How did you know?" she asked Ryan.

"Lucky guess."

"What a blessing for them," she said, her eyes on the happy couple as they accepted congratulatory hugs and kisses from the family. Yearning spread through Meghan, making her heart ache to hold Georgina.

Ryan pulled her close to his side. "Soon Georgina will be with us."

Us? "Did you talk to your dad?" The real possibility that the Fitzgeralds might want custody stirred her anxiety.

He shook his head. "Not yet. Tomorrow after church or Monday I'll sit him down and find out what he's thinking."

He didn't look too eager to do that. She could only imagine Ryan was still upset with his dad. She prayed he'd find a way to forgive his father so they could move on.

"Hey, I wanted to ask if you'd like to join the family for dinner tomorrow night," Ryan said.

Pleased by the invitation, she nodded. Maybe she had found more than just Georgina here in Fitzgerald Bay. Finally, she was finding a place to belong. Once they had Georgina with them, her world would be complete. "Yes. I'd love it."

Monday morning Meghan dressed in a tailored pantsuit and low heels for her meeting with the law firm of Schwartzmiller and Dean. She drove to Boston early, giving herself a buffer of time in case she ran into traffic. She hadn't expected the reply to her email query to result in such a quick meeting.

When she'd returned home yesterday from the church services, the reply had been waiting for her. Who knew law offices worked on the weekend? An unusual occurrence as far as she knew, but she wasn't complaining. She wanted the custody issued ASAP.

The email had listed information she needed to gather for her 9:00 a.m. meeting. That forced her to bow out of having dinner with Ryan and his family Sunday evening.

He'd understood, and to her excitement, asked her to have dinner with him Monday night. Just the two of them.

Life was looking up after the stress and trauma of the week before.

She parked in the law firm's parking garage. Clutching her file folder of requested information, she walked through the parking structure toward the elevator.

The squeal of tires echoed off the concrete walls.

"Watch out!" A woman stepping from the elevator shouted a warning.

Meghan turned to face a dark sedan barreling toward her. She barely jumped out of the way before the car streaked past.

"You okay?" the woman asked with concern.

Heart pumping and fear tightening her muscles, Meghan nodded. "Yeah, I'm okay." *If completely freaked out counted.* Was she being paranoid to think the driver of the car had deliberately tried to run her down?

"That guy was a total jerk," the woman muttered as she walked away to her own car.

On shaky legs, Meghan made her way upstairs. Once there she gave her name to the men at the front desk, then she was escorted through a metal detector and put on another elevator to the tenth floor.

Meghan was greeted by a fortysomething woman with red hair and stylish glasses perched on her nose. She held out her hand. "I'm Carol Marsden."

The name of the sender on the email that set the appointment. "Nice to meet you. I'm so glad you could meet with me today."

Carol laughed. "Not me, honey. One of the partners. Come along."

Meghan was surprised by that news. And curious. Why was a partner in one of Boston's biggest law firms interested in her custody case?

Carol led her to a conference room. "Mr. Dean will be right in." A pitcher of water and glasses sat on top of the oval mahogany table.

"Please help yourself to a glass of water." She gestured toward a sideboard with a pot of coffee steamed on a warmer next to a stack of ceramic mugs. "Or a cup of coffee."

Meghan sat in one of the leather captain's chairs, laid down her file folder and poured herself some water. Her hand shook. She took deep breaths to calm her racing heart. Ryan was sure Roman wouldn't come after her, especially in such a public way. There was no reason to think the incident in the parking garage was related to Christina, Georgina or Roman Wykoski. She remembered how she'd kept having the strange feeling she was being watched all weekend. Paranoid.

Still, she'd tell Ryan when she returned to Fitzgerald Bay.

A distinguished-looking man entered the room. He had to be in his sixties. His navy pin-striped suit and red tie screamed power. And money. Meghan swallowed, thankful this meeting was a free consultation.

"I'm Frank Dean," he said, holding out a manicured hand.

She rose to shake his hand. "Meghan Henry."

"Is this the information I requested?" He picked up the file folder.

"Yes."

He moved to a chair across from her and silently read through the contents of the folder. When he was done, he snapped it shut and stared at her.

Nerves had Meghan's foot tapping beneath the table.

"The letter is compelling," Dean finally said.

"My cousin's wish was that I raise her child."

"I understand Christina Hennessy has been arrested and is in jail."

"Yes, sir."

"I knew Burke," he admitted.

Ah. So that was why he was seeing her. "His death was a tragedy."

He nodded. "You do realize that seeking custody of Georgina Hennessy will be a challenge."

THIRTEEN

Meghan swallowed back the trepidation clogging her throat. "I'm up for it. I want her. I love her."

"Good. I know Burke loved her, too. It horrifies me that Christina killed him."

"She hasn't been convicted of the crime," Meghan said.

"True." He steepled his hands. "And not our concern here today. Gaining custody of Georgina is. There are some things that need to be set in place before we bring a custody motion before a judge."

"Like?"

"The most basic hurdle is you have no viable income. Freelance journalism hasn't netted you very much financial stability."

She winced. "I still have money from my parents' life insurance." Eventually those funds would run out, though. Something she'd known, but since she lived a frugal life as her parents had taught her, she hadn't ever been too worried about her finances, figuring when the time came, she'd step up her income.

"Which isn't enough to sustain you and Georgina for very long. Especially after you get my bill."

Her stomach sank.

"We need to have something more substantial to bring before the judge to prove you can provide for the child in question."

Blood pounded in her ears. "Like what?"

"The recent sale of a story that generates a decent wage and the possibility for future earnings. Or a job offer that will provide a steady income and benefits. Or you get married to a man with stable employment. Once that problem is solved, then we can move on to the others, which frankly aren't many."

She swallowed hard. Her mind raced. Good-paying jobs for more than an hourly rate were scarce in Fitzgerald Bay. She doubted waitressing at the Sugar Plum or scooping ice cream at the local parlor was what Mr. Dean had in mind. She'd have to return to Boston and pray she found something that would start right away and pay well. Her heart squeezed tight. She didn't want to leave Fitzgerald Bay. She liked the path her life was taking there.

But the alternative was unthinkable. She had to get custody of Georgina.

She could write the piece she'd already sketched out. The article could send her career on an income-generating path if CNN picked it up, like the editor at *Boston City News* hoped.

Or the last option was to get married.

There was only one man she'd consider for the job of husband. Ryan.

She'd fallen in love with him. She was ready to trust her heart and life to him. He was honorable and brave. A man of integrity. Gruff at times, but with a tender heart that made her feel safe and special.

But did he love her?

Cared for her, yes.

Found her attractive, she hoped so. The way he kissed her said he did.

But love?

They hardly knew each other. At least romantically. Chasing a madwoman across state lines and one social date didn't count as much of a courtship.

A marriage took time and commitment. A wedding couldn't just happen overnight, either.

Unless they eloped.

An elopement would solve everything. Well, if she had a willing groom. Doubts assailed her. What if Ryan didn't love her?

Then where would she be?

Back to the only real viable option. Writing the piece she'd promised to deliver to the editor at *Boston City News.*

She had to write the article. For Georgina. For herself. She couldn't risk not writing the piece.

She only hoped and prayed she wouldn't have to sell it.

Tonight, she would find out where she stood with Ryan. Then she'd know what she had to do.

Ryan arrived at Meghan's house a little before six with dinner from the Sugar Plum Café in a to-go bag. He'd decided he wanted to spend the evening alone with Meghan instead of in public view. Already people were linking them as a couple. And strangely he didn't mind.

He was falling for her, hook, line and sinker.

But he'd take it slow. She'd been hurt badly in the past. Something he never intended to do.

She opened the door to him with a beaming smile that took his breath away. He drew her close with his free hand. She laid her cheek against his chest. "I'm so happy to see you."

As welcomes went, this rated right up at the top. "I'm happy to see you, too."

She drew back. "Did you make your field trip to see Christina today?"

He shook his head. "No. They bumped her move

until tomorrow morning. I'll speak with her then. I have a feeling she'll stick to her story that Burke killed Olivia. She'll likely say he attacked both of them at the cliffs—and that's how her DNA ended up on the rock. We probably won't ever know for sure unless she confesses."

The news didn't sit well. She wanted justice for her cousin. If Burke did kill Olivia then his penance would be paid in the afterlife. But Meghan wanted to make Christina pay for her part in Olivia's death. "She could be let go?"

"No. The D.A. has enough evidence to convict on Burke's death. So either way, she's going to stay in prison for a long time."

"What about Mr. Sharp?"

He'd given them the lead that eventually made rescuing Georgina possible. It was only by the grace of God that Meghan and the children hadn't been hurt. She and Ryan had saved the children. There was no question in his mind that God had been with them. "Sharp's in general lockup at Rikers. He'll be staying."

"Good. Justice prevailed on that account." She hugged him again. He breathed in the clean scent of her shampoo. He was right where he wanted to be.

"Yum, that smells delicious." She stepped out of his arms. He wanted to pull her close again.

"I love that you brought dinner here," she said, taking the bag from him and heading toward the kitchen. "I'll put this on plates. The table's already set."

He glanced around, taking stock of her cottage. He'd admired the cottage from afar for along time. His own place just down the beach was a real money pit. A fixer-upper that he didn't have time to fix up. He could see the potential in the A-frame house but some days he couldn't get past the peeling paint, leaking pipes and ancient kitchen. But he much preferred Meghan's cozy house.

Everything had a lived-in look from the floral couch, the Queen Anne chair to the round oak dining table near the window. Vases full of fresh flowers added an extra cheeriness to the antique furnishings.

He heard the bang of cupboards and the clank of dishes. "Can I help?" he called out.

"No. Just have a seat," she called back.

He moved toward the dining table near the side picture window. In the light of day there would be a nice view of the ocean. Tonight, however, only darkness lay beyond the glass pane.

A laptop sitting open precariously close to the edge of a couch cushion, as if hastily set aside, drew his attention. Meghan must have been working. He nudged it to place it in a more secure position and the screen lit up.

The headline and byline snagged his attention.

Baby Smuggling and the Fitzgerald Bay Connection

By Meghan Henry.

Hardly daring to breathe, let alone believe what he was seeing, Ryan read the article. Horror grew with each word. When he'd finished reading, he sank down onto the couch, feeling boneless.

The story painted a sad picture of a young girl reaching out in desperation to the father she never knew. And that man, her father—Ryan's father—Aiden Fitzgerald, the man running for mayor of Fitzgerald Bay—refused to help his illegitimate daughter, thus sending the girl on a doomed path. The story continued on, chronicling the events leading to the arrest of socialite Christina Hennessy and the rescue of three innocent lives from human traffickers.

The words blurred on the screen. His eyes burned. The double-edged sword of betrayal sliced through his heart. The hurt was raw and jagged. The anger he'd felt for his father rose with a vengeance.

Along with a new anger.

Meghan, his Meghan, had written an exposé that could destroy his family.

In his eyes, that was unforgivable.

Meghan returned to the living room carrying a tray laden with steaming plates of chicken Parmesan, sides of broccoli and rice and a basket of sourdough rolls. Ryan sat on the couch. In his hands was her laptop. The ice frosting his gaze sent a chill down her spine. She stopped abruptly. A piece of broccoli bounced off a plate and disappeared beneath the couch.

"You can't do this," he said, his voice hard and cold.

Fighting back the sudden fear that griped her, she stepped forward. Ryan was not like her exhusband. He would not take out his anger on her.

Slowly, she set down the tray on the coffee table. "Let me explain."

He jumped to his feet. "You mean explain how you shoved a knife into my back."

Heart pounding, she held her ground and contemplated how best to diffuse the situation. "I saw a lawyer today. He suggested—"

"That you destroy my family?"

"No." She reached out for him. He jerked back. Hurt, she let her hand drop to her side. "He said I need to show an income from my writing if I have any hope of gaining custody of Georgina." She planned to tell him this over their dinner. This and that she loved him and wanted to spend the rest of her life with him. "The editor at *Boston City News* will pay handsomely for this article."

"There has to be another way than this... this garbage."

His words ripped into her. Her defenses rose. She didn't think bringing up the other option of marriage would go over well now. "The public deserves to know the whole story before they elect Aiden to the mayor's seat."

"The way you spin this, you make him out to be a monster."

"I only wrote what I know to be true."

"The truth is more complicated than this." He snapped the laptop closed and tossed it onto the couch. "What about us, Meghan?"

The tortured expression on his face hammered at her resolve.

"I love you," she admitted, hating how hollow the words sounded. Nothing like the way she'd pictured declaring her love for him.

He scoffed. "And this is how you show it?"

"This isn't about you. I need a way to support Georgina. I'm a journalist, Ryan. I write what needs to be told." She had to make him understand that she had to do this. "I have to submit this, Ryan. My editor has promised me the front page. If CNN picks it up—"

"CNN?" he groaned and fell back a step.

"It could make the difference in the custody hearing. I'm a single woman. I need to show that I can financially provide for Georgina."

"And you think the way to do that is by destroying my family. Her family."

Meghan sucked in a sharp breath. "Your father turned his back on her. On Olivia."

"Please, don't do this." In two long strides he closed the distance between them. "I'm begging you, please don't do this."

Her heart lurched at the idea that this big, proud man would beg for anything. Maybe there was a chance they could salvage their relationship. If he could only see this from her point of view. "Ryan—"

He took her hand and held on tight. "You'll drag us all through the mud. Georgina included. Think about her. Think about how this will affect her growing up if all the world knows the horrible details of her birth and her mother."

He didn't play fair.

"I'll protect her."

He dropped his hand. The chill in his gaze returned, freezing in its intensity. "You won't be able to protect her from the gossip and rumors. She'll always live under a cloud if you print this story."

"We don't live in the eighteenth century, Ryan. It may feel that way sometimes living in this quaint town with its tight-knit community, but scandals come and go. No one blinks an eye at illegitimate children these days."

The sad testament of the world's moral status

didn't appear to appease him, if the glare he leveled on her was any indication.

"This is more about how the scandal will affect *you* not her."

His scowl darkened. "Your story is more important than family," he shot back.

She stiffened, feeling like he'd slapped her. "The only family I have left is Georgina. I can't let her down or Olivia." She had no options left now. He'd ridiculed her declaration of love. He was angry and hurt. She tried not to take offense but it stung anyway.

"You're letting me down," he ground out.

His words cut deep. "Do you love me?" she asked.

His icy silence was answer enough. Her heart cracked in her chest, pain seared her soul as any chance of happiness with Ryan slipped away.

Tears gathered, but she refused to let him see her cry. "Georgina and I will move away. Go someplace where no one has heard of Fitzgerald Bay or the Fitzgeralds."

Hurt crossed his handsome features before a mask of stone settled into place. "No, you won't. She's our family, too. I'll make sure you never receive custody of her."

Shock ripped the breath from her lungs. "You wouldn't do that! You couldn't. You know how much I love her. How much Olivia wanted me to have her."

He headed to the front door. "Prove you love her. Don't write the article."

With that he was gone.

Meghan sank to the floor, more afraid than she'd ever been. She'd come this far, gone through so much, to find Georgina. Now Ryan threatened to keep Georgina from her.

It wasn't fair.

The crevices in her heart opened wider. She'd lost Ryan.

She couldn't lose Georgina, too.

Ryan had to warn his father. As angry as he was at him, the reasons stacking up like driftwood blown into Fitzgerald Bay by as many nor'easters, Ryan couldn't let his father be blindsided by the scandal.

By Meghan's betrayal.

Ryan hurt deep inside. A pain so breath-stealing, he'd rather have seven cracked ribs than feel this sort of emotional torment.

This late in the evening, Ryan knew where to find his father. A few minutes later, Ryan entered the house he'd grown up in and made his way to the kitchen where Dad sat eating the dinner Mrs. Mulrooney, Dad's housekeeper, had made for him.

He wore casual clothes that hung on him. Unbidden concern for his dad pricked his mind. Aiden had lost weight and there were newer, deeper lines around his eyes.

Aiden's eyebrows arched as Ryan slid into the chair across the table from him.

"Hello, son." Aidan set down his fork. "This is a pleasant surprise. I thought you had dinner plans with Meghan."

Ryan's teeth clenched against the fresh wave of hurt. He should be having dinner with Meghan, getting to know each other better without bullets flying. He'd envisioned a moonlight walk on the beach, holding hands, maybe even kissing....

"Dad, we have a situation." He explained Meghan's article and the damage it would do.

Aiden sat back, folded his hands over his chest and stared silently up at the ceiling.

Frustrated by the lack of reaction, Ryan said, "Dad, did you hear me? This could ruin your chances of becoming mayor."

He flicked a glance Ryan's way. "And your chances of stepping into the chief's spot."

Ryan blinked. The next step in the equation hadn't occurred to him. Sure, he'd been working toward the goal of being chief, but he didn't care about that right now. After the past few days, he was more inclined to let someone else take the chief's spot. He much preferred being out in the field.

Aiden heaved a heavy sigh and turned his pale blue eyes on Ryan. "From what it sounds like, this article Meghan has written is nothing but the truth. You shouldn't be upset."

Ryan drew back. "Not be upset? How can you be so blasé? This will affect all of us. Your bid for mayor will die a flaming death. The reputation of the family will be tarnished. Everything we do as men of the law will be questioned."

This is more about how the scandal will affect you not her.

Meghan's words slammed into him with a vicious blow. His mouth turned to cotton. Was that true? His mind recoiled from looking too closely at her words and his reaction to them.

Determination set Dad's jaw in a firm line. "It's time I took responsibility for my actions, my mistakes."

"A little late for that now," Ryan muttered. Anger at his dad's disloyalty to his mom and resentment for not being the man Ryan had thought his dad was and sorrow for all the heartache his father's actions had caused made his chest tighten. He rubbed the spot over his heart with one hand.

Aiden clasped Ryan's other hand. "Can you ever forgive me?"

The words knifed through him, making his eyes

burn and his lungs feel like they were collapsing. The walls of the kitchen closed in, the very air around him was devoid of oxygen. He felt trapped, cornered. "I don't know. I—just don't know, Dad."

FOURTEEN

Ryan had to get out of there. Away from his dad, away from the pain burrowing deep, trying to drag him into a pit so dark he wasn't sure there would be a way out. Without another word, he rose and fled from the house.

He bypassed his vehicle and walked all the way to the beach. A path he and his siblings had taken many times growing up. Always before, the anticipation of fun in the sun had made the walk easy. Today the distance felt like miles and miles of torture.

He nodded to folks out for an evening stroll. Normally he'd stop and ask how they were doing. But not today. His mind was in turmoil. Every physical injury he'd suffered this past week throbbed. His heart lay heavy in his chest and his soul burdened.

He hit the beach, immediately shucking his shoes and socks and rolling up his pant legs. The loose sand was cool beneath his feet. He walked down to the water, the shore turning hard and wet. Waves lapped at his ankles as he treaded through the foaming ocean.

Finally he let the thoughts rattling around his brain form, examining and analyzing them with careful consideration.

Dad had been unfaithful to Mom. He'd kept Olivia a secret from his children.

Can you ever forgive me?

Dad's question hammered at Ryan. A war waged within his soul. Bitterness and anger versus love.

Forgiveness is the way to freedom from that which binds us.

Meghan's voice invaded his head, adding to the fray. Words he'd thought trite now hit him profoundly. He was bound by anger. Betrayal. Hurt.

By his father.

By Meghan.

Only you can choose to forgive.

A process, Meghan had said. How did he even begin?

Lord, I don't know what to do. What to pray. I'm so full of anger and hurt. I want to forgive...I don't even know how.

Ryan lifted his gaze toward the town. Lights illuminated the peak of the white spire of the Fitzgerald Bay Community Church. A beacon saying, "Come here."

With a sense of urgency Ryan didn't completely

understand, he gathered his shoes, quickly donned them and then hustled for the church and the solace he hoped to find there.

This evening the church was empty and quiet. The interior of the building was still softly lit with candles and low-wattage lighting glowed from wall sconces attached to wooden beams. The same paintings—depicting ships leaving the harbor with sailors setting out on the dangerous oceans, never knowing if they'd return—graced the walls since he was a kid as reminders to pray for the town and its seafaring people.

Thick oak pews lined the sanctuary. At the front of the church, colorful stained-glass windows provided a beautiful background to the plain wooden cross recessed on the stage where Pastor Larch usually preached. The simplicity of the cross beckoned Ryan forward until he reached the first pew. He slipped onto the bench and lifted his gaze to the cross.

He wasn't sure what he hoped to find here. Clarity. Peace of mind. Forgiveness.

"Ryan?"

Ryan swiveled to see Pastor Larch coming down the aisle. Ryan stood. "Hi, Pastor. Hope it's okay I'm here because it's not Sunday morning."

Pastor Larch gave him an indulgent smile. "God's house is always open, Ryan, regardless of the day. Please, sit."

Ryan sat back down where he'd been. Pastor Larch slid onto the bench next to him.

For a moment they were silent, each staring up at the cross.

Ryan felt the pastor's gaze on him. He realized what he must look like. Hair mussed from the ocean's wind, pants wet, wrinkled and sandy from being shoved up before wading in the water. A haunted look in his eyes.

"You seem troubled," Pastor Larch stated.

Troubled. What a mild word for the chaos going on inside him. "Family stuff."

"Do you want to talk about it?"

"Not really." But then why was he here?

The need to speak rose sharply, forcing words past the lump in his throat. Ryan poured out all the agony that cluttered his head and heart and soul. He confessed to the anger he felt toward his father, the hurt Meghan's article had caused and questioned how he could move past it all. Pastor Larch listened attentively, offering words of wisdom and encouragement.

When he finished with his tale, Ryan felt drained, depleted and achy.

"Meghan's right, you know. Forgiveness doesn't always come easy. But it's worth the effort, every single struggle, to get to a place where you can pray for the person who hurt you rather than condemn them."

Ryan remembered the passage in Matthew where Jesus taught His disciples to bless and pray for your enemies. Though Ryan didn't necessarily view his father as his enemy, the gist of the teaching spoke to him.

"How do I begin?" Ryan asked.

"With prayer."

So simple. Doable. Yet the words wouldn't form. He'd spent so much time in the past questioning God, questioning other people's faith. After sending his best friend, who'd professed to be a man of God, to jail for abusing his girlfriend, Ryan's own faith had slipped. Over the past week it had returned like a tide, ebbing and flowing. He wasn't sure where he stood at the moment. He wanted to grab on to his faith. He really did.

"There are times when our own offended pride, more than hurt or anger, blocks us from God," Pastor Larch gently pointed out.

Something deep inside Ryan grew agitated. He'd never thought of himself as prideful.

This is more about how the scandal will affect you not her.

Everything inside of him stilled. His heart, his breath. He searched to the depths of his soul. With a sinking feeling of shame and grief, he realized the pastor was right. Meghan had been right. His own pride underlined his hurt and anger, preventing him from praying, from forgiving. From loving Meghan.

Ryan bowed his head. "Forgive me, Lord. Take my pride, fill me with Your love."

Pastor Larch laid a hand on Ryan's shoulder and prayed for him, for his family. His kind words, his compassionate voice wrapped around Ryan as if God himself was hugging him. Tears burned Ryan's eyes as he let God's healing begin.

Help me forgive my father, Lord, he silently asked of God. *I can't do it on my own.*

He could physically feel his heart soften. Clarity rushed in, crowding out all the bad stuff that had kept him from seeing the truth.

His father was human and had made mistakes. God loved him despite his sins. Could Ryan do no less?

In such a short span of time so much had transpired, so much had changed. And with it, so had Ryan.

No longer was he afraid to feel, afraid to open up and let emotion in. The battle in his soul had been won. Love triumphed. Love for his family.

Love for Meghan.

Hopefully, she'd give him another chance.

The next morning Ryan awoke to the ringing of his cell phone. The caller ID told him Douglas was on the line.

"Hey," he said by way of an answer.

"You'd better get down to the courthouse, pronto. Dad's arranged for a press conference."

Scrambling from his bed, he said, "I'll be right there."

Looked like Dad was standing behind his words. Aiden was going to take responsibility for his actions. Ryan knew the sacrifice his father was making. Pride, the good kind, filled him. It didn't matter that his father's confession would come on the heels of the article Meghan probably submitted last night. Dad was doing the right thing.

Ryan dressed and shaved quickly, then made his way down Main Street, noting that a crowd had gathered outside the courthouse, which sat adjacent to the Fitzgerald Bay police station. All of his siblings were present as were his cousins and aunts and uncles. The whole Fitzgerald-Connolly clan had turned out to support Aiden. Had his father told them what he was about to do? Had he explained that the announcement he was about to make would be a death knell for the upcoming mayoral election?

Camera crews and journalists crowded around the steps of the courthouse. Ryan slipped in line beside his sister Fiona. She stood proud and tall, in a subdued green dress that showed off her red hair. She grabbed his hand and held on tight. Emotion clogged Ryan's throat as his father addressed the hovering crowd.

Listening to his father talk of his past and the mistakes he had made since were hard to hear, but the truth didn't hurt nearly as badly as it had when Meghan had first shed light upon his father's misdeeds.

"My heartfelt apologies go out to the citizens of Fitzgerald Bay. I acted selfishly," Aiden said, concluding his speech.

Hands rose, demanding attention. Questions were lobbed at the chief of police. Aiden answered each with patience and grace, making Ryan proud.

A flash of honey-blond hair caught Ryan's attention. Meghan stood at the back of the crowd. She wore a becoming sunny-yellow dress and low-heeled sandals. Dark sunglasses hid her eyes.

The sight of her jump-started his pulse. The love he'd been denying expanded in his chest until he could hardly breathe. He owed her an apology. A lifetime's worth for his bad behavior. He'd been cruel. Said something he had no intention of following through on. Lashed out over the article she'd written. He couldn't take Georgina away from her.

The uncharacteristic loss of control shook him. Only this woman could do that to him. Meghan. His Meghan.

There was so much he wanted to say to her. He

need to tell her she'd done the right thing in bringing the truth to light. Her integrity filled him with pride and respect and admiration and…so many other emotions he felt he might burst with them all. Determination to win her love filled him.

"I'll be back," he whispered into Fiona's ear as he withdrew his hand.

He threaded his way through the crowd, but lost sight of Meghan. When he got to the place where she'd been standing, she was gone. He searched the crowd and caught sight of her entering the park. "Meghan," he shouted.

She continued walking. He wasn't sure if she truly hadn't heard him or was ignoring him. He wouldn't blame her if she ignored him. He'd been a jerk to her.

"Ryan Fitzgerald, tell us about capturing Christina Hennessy." A reporter jabbed a microphone at Ryan.

"Has DNA proven that Georgina Hennessy is a Fitzgerald?" another voice in the crowd asked.

Ryan watched Meghan walk out of sight. He sighed. He'd have to wait until the press conference was over to talk with her.

Meghan Henry had wormed her way into Ryan's heart. He only hoped she'd give him a chance to prove himself to her. Prove he was a man worth taking a chance on, worth loving. He'd made her promises. Promises he intended to keep.

* * *

Meghan walked listlessly through town, past the ice cream shop, past the bookstore and the pharmacy. A chill chased down her spine despite the warm June humidity. She stopped and spun around. No one was paying her any attention. Still…she should have told Ryan about almost being run down yesterday, but the evening had turned into a disaster before she'd had a chance.

When she'd seen the email notice pop up this morning about the impromptu press conference called by the Fitzgerald Bay police chief, she'd hardly believed it. She'd hurried to the courthouse along with more than half the town and journalists in this part of the state. She appreciated that Aiden Fitzgerald had finally and very publicly taken ownership of his part in her cousin's life and death.

She ached for what it would cost him and his family. Contrary to what Ryan thought, she cared about them all. About Ryan. She was sure Ryan blamed her, probably hated her. The thought was like a knife to the chest.

Ryan hadn't even tried to talk to her at the press conference. He'd stared at her from his place behind his father like a stone statue. His inscrutable eyes revealed nothing. She might as well not exist to him. She supposed she didn't.

Heartsick, she couldn't deny she loved Ryan Fitzgerald and he didn't love her back.

His last words to her echoed flatly inside her chest.

She's our family, too. I'll make sure you never receive custody of her.

If he'd loved her, he wouldn't have said those horrible words. He didn't love her. A sad fact she had to accept.

She'd known falling in love again was madness. Had thought she'd never go down this road again but then she hadn't figured on Ryan Fitzgerald. He'd gotten past the barricades she'd erected around her heart. Made her think her heart was safe with him.

But he'd hurt her. Not physically as her ex had. Ryan would never be that guy.

This hurt went deeper and made her bleed inside.

She headed back to her lonely cottage by the sea. There was no question she had to leave Fitzgerald Bay. Being here hurt too much. Seeing Ryan hurt too much.

Even though she'd turned in an article that she was proud of, it wasn't the one Ryan had read. After he'd left she'd taken a good long look at her work and viewed the story from Ryan's point of view. She hadn't like what she'd read. The words sounded vindictive and crushing.

Not the person she wanted to be.

So she'd revised the story to reflect the heroism of a certain deputy chief and the rescue of innocent lives.

As a freelance journalist Meghan knew there would be other stories, other chances to gain recognition and higher wages.

What she needed at the moment was to show a judge that she had a steady income and stable home to provide for Georgina. And that meant heading back to Boston and finding a well-paying job. Now.

Her lawyer, Mr. Dean, had said she could visit Georgina soon. The only bright spot in a rather dismal week.

When she arrived at her cottage, she dragged her suitcase from the hall closet and laid it open on the blue-and-red toile printed comforter and began systematically packing her clothing. As she emptied each drawer and slid it shut, the hollow sound echoed in the stillness of the cottage, magnifying the hollow feeling in her heart.

What would Ryan think when he read her revised article today?

She wouldn't be here to find out.

A noise stilled her hands. Was that a knock she'd heard? Hope flared. Had Ryan had a change of heart and come to see her? She hurried to the door trying not to let her expectations fly too high.

Wood splintered as the front door gave way to the man forcing his way in.

Terror crashed over Meghan, engulfing her in its smothering intensity like a tsunami wiping out everything in its wake. A scream tore from her lungs. She turned to flee, to find an escape.

Roman Wykoski grabbed her by the hair and yanked her backward. Dragging her out the front door, he growled, "You thought you were so smart, you and your boyfriend. No one makes a fool of me and lives."

Frantic, Meghan kicked and screamed as he hauled her from the cottage.

Please, God, save me.

Despair underscored the terror. No one would come looking for her. Georgina would grow up without her. No one else would miss her.

Especially not Ryan.

FIFTEEN

Ryan saw his father slip away. After the press conference the family was gathered in the living room of the family home. Ryan followed his dad to the study.

The sounds of his siblings muted as he closed the door behind him. "I'm proud of you, Dad."

His father's confession of his affair, his mistakes since and his heartfelt apology to his family and the town rang with sincerity. Humbly taking ownership of his faults had endeared him to his family. And Ryan hoped to the town.

Aiden sat in the recliner by the window. His favorite reading spot. "Thank you, son. That means a lot to me."

As a young boy, Ryan used to love to climb onto his dad's lap and listen to him read from the stack of books Ryan would drag in. The memory evoked affection. For all his faults, Aiden Fitzgerald had been a good dad to him. "I owe you an apology, Dad."

Aiden shook his head. "No."

"Yes. I let my anger and hurt cloud what's important." Family, loyalty, love.

"I wish I'd done things differently. I wish I'd exercised better judgment."

"The past is over and done with," Ryan stated, remembering when Meghan had shared this wisdom with him. He hadn't bought it then, but now he understood. Dwelling on what had already been only robbed him of what could be. "We have to figure out how to live in the now, then the future."

"When did you become so wise?" his father asked.

Ryan couldn't claim the credit. "Since I allowed Meghan Henry into my life."

His father arched a gray speckled eyebrow. "Ah. The lovely Meghan. You care about her."

So much more than cared. "Yes. I love her."

"Have you told her?"

Ryan heaved a heavy sigh full of self-recrimination and guilt. "No."

In fact she probably thought he despised her. Which was far from the truth. "Dad, Meghan wants custody of Georgina."

"I thought she might," Aiden said. "It's what Olivia wanted."

"Can you help make it happen?"

Aiden smiled. "I'll see what I can do."

A wave of relief lifted some of the weight bearing down on him. "Georgina's in emergency foster care. Probably scared and confused. It'd sure be nice if we could get her to Meghan sooner rather than later," Ryan said, hoping his father would take action.

His father glanced at his watch. "I have a few favors I can call in. And she is my granddaughter."

And Ryan's niece. "Thanks, Dad."

His father waved a hand. "Go to Meghan. Tell her how you feel."

"I will."

The study door open. Keira rushed in, her eyes wide and panicked. "Dad, Ryan."

Her agitation knotted Ryan's gut. "What's happened?"

"Christina Hennessy's transport was ambushed. She's escaped."

Ryan drove to Meghan's. He wanted her to hear the news of Christina's escape from him. Though he'd had a patrol car drive by often, he still needed to make sure she was safe. He parked in front of her cottage, jumped out of his rig and hurried up the walkway.

A stray sandal lay on the ground. A sense of foreboding prickled the tiny hairs at the base of his neck.

He picked it up, frowning at the shoe. Hadn't

Meghan been wearing this at the press conference? A knot of apprehension fisted his gut.

The front door of the cottage was ajar. The splintered wood and broken lock sent a shock of fear jolting through him. Caution made him reach for his holstered weapon at his side. Leading with his gun, he entered the cottage.

"Meghan!"

The end table lay on its side. The contents of Meghan's purse lay scattered on the floor. The area rug was bunched up. All signs of a struggle.

He locked down all emotion and grabbed his phone. He called his brother Douglas and explained the situation. As he talked he did a quick sweep of the house even though he knew she wouldn't be there. Someone had taken her. The sight of the half-filled suitcase on her bed disturbed him but he couldn't let his mind even process that, not when every instinct told him she was in danger.

"We'll find her, bro," Douglas said. "I'll send everyone out. We'll canvass the area, see if anyone saw something."

Ryan stepped out on the porch. There were few houses at this end of the beach. His own place was barely visible a quarter of a mile down the shore. "I'm going to check the beach."

The flutter of paper drew his attention. An ice

pick stabbed a note to the porch railing. "Wait a sec. I found something."

He read the scrawled note. His heart dropped. His self-control crumbled. Panic throbbed in his head. Wykoski had Meghan. The note instructed Ryan to come alone to the cliffs off the Fitzgerald Bay lighthouse if he wanted to see Meghan alive. The same place where they'd found Olivia Henry's broken body.

"What is it?" Douglas asked.

Ryan lifted his gaze and scanned the street, the beach, the ocean. Was he being watched?

"Wykoski's got her." Terror twisted him up inside. His chest squeezed tight until drawing breath was difficult. He jogged to his rig and climbed inside. With tires squealing, he roared down the street. "He wants me to come to the lighthouse cliffs if I want to see her again."

"You stay put. I'll be right there. We'll go together," Douglas said in a firm tone.

"No time. Already en route. I need to save her. Meet me there." Ryan hung up and concentrated on driving to the place where this nightmare began.

A terrifying image slammed into his consciousness. An image of Meghan, broken and bleeding at the bottom of the cliffs.

His heart in his throat, Ryan sent up an urgent prayer.

God save her. Help me save her.

He'd just found the love of his life. Losing her now would be a blow his heart would never recover from.

The sound of the tires against asphalt reverberated in her ears. Her eyes had finally adjusted to the darkness. But her heart cried out against the stiffling confines of the trunk she'd been forced into. She had no idea where Roman was taking her. She was almost afraid to find out.

Meghan prayed fervently, silently. *Help me, Lord. Please help me.*

She lay curled in a fetal position. Plastic ties bound her wrists painfully behind her back. More ties secured her feet together. A foul-tasting cloth stretched across her mouth. She drew in air through her nose. But she couldn't get enough oxygen. She felt suffocation clawing at her, sending her already frightened senses careening. Beneath her the car vibrated as the tires sped along the pavement.

The car slowed, leaving smooth road for a bumpy, gravel drive. She shifted in the trunk, her hip hitting something hard, the jack, maybe a box of tire chains. Rocks pinged off the undercarriage. Each hit felt like a slap or the ticking of a clock.

Oh, Ryan, if only...

The car jerked to a stop. Her heart lurched.

For a moment all was quiet. Except the pounding of her heart. She concentrated. She faintly heard the sound of the ocean crashing on shore, the clang of a buoy marking shallow water. The ocean, but she could be anywhere along the eastern seaboard at this point.

Roman's threat swirled through her mind, beating down what little hope remained in her heart.

Did he plan to put her on a boat and take her away to sell her as he'd threatened before? Or did he plan to kill her and dispose of her body in the ocean?

The trunk lid popped open. Bright light surrounded her. Blinded her. Meghan winced.

Through squinty eyes, she made out her captor's silhouette. Rough hands dragged her from the trunk, her stiff and aching body banging with painful thuds against the lip of the trunk, then the bumper, until finally landing in a heap on the ground. Sharp-edged rocks bit into her flesh. Tears stung her eyes. She cried out, but no one could hear her.

Overhead a gull screeched, its cry echoing the scream trapped behind Meghan's gag.

She glanced around.

Her heart pounded. She knew this place.

They were parked off the main road leading to the Fitzgerald Bay lighthouse. Roman hadn't taken her far at all. This was the place where Olivia's body had been found.

The reality of her own fate became crystal clear at that moment. Meghan's stomach knotted, threatening to upheave the bile churning inside.

He wasn't going to sell her. Otherwise, he wouldn't want her so beat-up and bruised. No, he was going to kill her.

Self-preservation kept her calm. If she didn't do something, she would die. She'd never see Ryan or baby Georgina again.

Roman lifted her in his arms and carried her past the white-and-red-striped lighthouse. She bucked and twisted. Frantic fear clouded her mind.

Unperturbed by her struggling, he followed the path that led to the edge of the jagged bluff. Wind whistled up the wall of stone carrying the briny scent of the water crashing on the ragged rocks below. Was he going to throw her over the cliff?

Please, God, no!

At the edge, he dumped her from his arms onto the loose, crumbling earth. Rocks and stones slid down the face of the cliff. She shuddered, scooting back from the edge as best she could. She whimpered with terror.

"Now what?" a woman's strident voice demanded.

Shock snapped Meghan from the debilitating fear. Someone else was here. She arched her body to see who was behind her.

Christina Hennessy stood several paces away. Meghan sucked in a sharp breath.

Wait. Christina was supposed to be in jail. Meghan tried to make sense of the situation.

Wind whipped her blond hair into a frenzy. She wore a bright orange jumper. Prison garb. How had she escaped? Why was she with Roman Wykoski?

"We wait," Roman said. "He'll show up and then we'll take care of them both."

Did Roman mean Ryan would show up? Roman was planning an ambush on Ryan.

"He won't come alone," Christina warned. "Just dump her over the side and let's go. You promised me we could leave."

"No worries, sis. I'm prepared. Our escape route is all set."

Sis? As in siblings? Meghan's mind tried to make sense of it.

Prepared? A fresh stab of fear pierced through her. Her heart wept for the man she loved. He would come to rescue her but walk into a trap. There was no way for her to warn him.

Oh, God, please, protect him.

Ryan parked a half mile from the lighthouse. He didn't know what Wykoski had planned but Ryan wasn't walking into a trap. He approached the lighthouse by way of the bay, taking cover in the trees and scrub grass dotting the beach.

Up ahead to his right, he saw a man lying in the grass with a sniper's rifle aimed toward the cliffs above. A short distance offshore a dingy bobbed in the water.

Stealthily, Ryan crept closer until he was within striking distance of the sniper. He planted a foot in the man's back. Snaked his arm around the guy's neck and squeezed, cutting off his oxygen supply.

A moment later, the man slumped, unconscious in Ryan's arm. He laid him facedown. Liberating the rifle, Ryan ducked behind a boulder and used the rifle's scope to assess the situation at the top of the cliff.

Meghan lay on the ground near the edge of the cliff, bound and gagged. But alive. He let out a ragged breath of relief.

For now.

Fierce anger surged through Ryan. He had to save her.

He sighted in on Roman pacing nearby.

Ryan's finger twitched.

Roman stopped and seemed to speak to someone out of view.

In the distance, sirens wailed. Roman jerked toward the sound. A grim smile broke over Roman's evil face.

Unease slithered down Ryan's back. He needed to get closer.

In a low crouch, he ran for the road, crossed and then found a spot on higher ground behind a maple tree. Again using the scope, he surveyed the situation.

At the cliff's edge, Roman stood over Meghan. Standing next to him was…Christina Hennessy.

Ryan's jaw dropped.

Nothing was what it seemed. He scanned the horizon.

Sunlight glinted off another shooter's scope two hundred yards left of the lighthouse. He continued to the left and right. Another gunman lay behind a bush near Charles's cottage. Roman was leaving nothing to chance.

Ryan sent up a silent prayer of thanksgiving that his brother Charles and kids were safe at Dad's house and not at home in the lighthouse keeper's residence.

His gaze zeroed in on something on the lighthouse balcony overlooking the road. A third sniper.

Fear sent him frantically reaching for his phone. He yanked it from his pocket and called Douglas.

"It's a trap," Ryan warned in tight whisper. "You and the others back off. I'll deal with this."

"No way!" Douglas shouted. "I'm coming whether you want me there or not."

Meghan's life was at stake. He didn't have time

to argue. Ryan relayed the position of each un-identified suspect. "Christina is here. Roman is holding Meghan at the edge of the cliff. She looks injured."

His heart squeezed tight. He wanted another chance with her. To apologize. To tell her…

"I'll inform the others," Douglas said. "Don't take any chances."

Ryan clicked off with out answering. That wasn't a promise he could make.

The woman he loved was in danger. He wasn't going to stand around and let her be harmed.

Meghan fought against the fear threatening to swallow her whole. She couldn't give in to it, in to the dark shadows closing in on her mind. She'd accepted her fate. But the sirens drew Ryan closer and closer to an ambush. She wouldn't accept anything happening to him. She had to do something, had to keep him safe, even if it cost her in the end. She wouldn't let the man she loved die.

Her hand closed over a loose, jagged stone. This might work.

She wedged it between her wrists. All she had to do was work the nylon tie around her wrist against it. In theory it sounded easy. Reality…remained to be seen. She prayed this worked. She rolled toward Christina, mindful of the long drop below.

Christina jumped as if she'd been poked with a hot stick.

Roman laughed. "She can't hurt you."

To cover up her intentions, Meghan screamed questions, made unintelligible by the cloth wedged between her lips. She rocked side to side as she screamed, using the rock like a saw against the tie.

Christina yanked the gag away from Meghan's mouth. "I take it you want to talk."

Gulping in air, Meghan swallowed and nearly retched on the disgusting taste on her tongue. "Why are you doing this?"

Christina's eyes glittered with an insane kind of fervor. "You interfered in our business. Now we have to leave. Start over somewhere else. You have to pay the price for your meddling."

Hating to think what that price might be, Meghan asked, "How did you escape from prison?"

Mouth curling, Christina sneered. "Really? How do you think? Roman broke me out."

Of course Roman broke her out. It just seemed so impossible. Unreal. "So he's your brother."

Heaving a beleaguered sigh, Christina nodded. "Yep. Two years older. Genetics. What can you do?"

Meghan had so many questions. "I guess that also might explain why you killed Burke."

A shuttered look came over Christina's face. "I

had no choice but to kill him. When he found out I had killed Olivia, he was going to turn me in. He was going to betray his own wife."

Meghan stilled. Surprise siphoned the blood from her brain, making the world tilt. Blinding grief brought tears to Meghan's eyes. Finally she knew definitively who killed her cousin. "Why did you kill her?"

"She wanted to take my baby away from me. She said she'd changed her mind and wanted to take sweet Georgina back. I couldn't let that happen."

Christina's hands fisted. "She fought me. Scratched my arm like a wild cat. Drew blood even. I lost my favorite dolphin charm."

She sounded put out about the loss of her jewelry. "When I saw the picture of me wearing the charm on the wall at the Sugar Plum I knew someone would recognize it and connect it to me. Then when the police showed the charm on the television I had to run."

The pieces all fell into place. "So that's when you decided to give Georgina to your brother to sell? Why would you do that?"

She made a face. "Not the best move. I wasn't thinking straight."

Meghan blinked. As opposed to the straight thinking that led her to murder? The woman was certifiable.

Three loud rapid-fire gunshots split the air. Meghan flinched and ducked her head into the dirt.

Christina screamed. Roman cursed and hit the ground.

Frantic, Meghan inched her way farther from the cliff, while the sharp-edged stone tore at the binding. She could feel the tie loosen. *Please, God. Help me.*

"Roman!" Christina cried, clutching at him.

He rose and ran toward Meghan. "To the cliff, hurry!" he yelled. "There's a rope. Climb down."

Christina raced for the bluff. She grabbed a coiled rope tethered to a spike in the ground that Meghan hadn't seen and tossed it over the side.

Roman grabbed Meghan's legs. He dragged her toward the edge. His fingers dug into her skin. Pebbles poked and scraped her back. She screamed, "No!"

The bindings around her wrists gave. She clawed at him.

A shot rang out.

Meghan screamed.

Roman dropped her legs. His body jerked backward, his feet coming off the ground. He landed faceup with a gaping hole in his chest.

Meghan struggled to her knees.

Strong arms lifted her to her feet.

Fresh fear jolted her system. She fought to be free.

"Meghan, honey, its me," a familiar male voice said.

Ryan!

Relief flooded her. She sagged against him as sobs racked her body. "You're safe."

"I'm safe." He hugged her tightly. "You're safe. Roman's dead. You don't have to worry about him ever again."

She pulled away from him and gazed into his eyes. "But Christina!"

"Didn't get far," he said, gesturing to where his brothers Douglas and Owen were hauling Christina back onto stable ground.

"Let me go," Christina screamed.

"She killed Olivia and Burke." Meghan hiccuped, her tears slowly drying. Ryan cut the ties at her ankles. "Roman was her brother."

Ryan's eyebrows rose. "Cooper was right. The family's crazy."

"I didn't think I'd ever see you again." She clutched his shoulders. She could hardly believe he was real. "I was so afraid."

"I was, too." His hands spanned her waist. His touch was so tender, so comforting. "When I arrived at your house and saw that someone had broken in, I thought I'd lost you. I don't ever want to lose you, Meghan. I love you."

Delight exploded in her heart. "You do?"

"I do." Contrition marred his brow. "Can you ever forgive me for acting like such a jerk?"

She cupped his face in her hands. She didn't have to think about it, the answer came readily. "Yes, I can forgive you. I love you, Ryan Fitzgerald. More than I can possibly say."

Joy spread across his handsome face. "You don't know how happy that makes me feel."

His lips captured hers. Hope filled her heart and love poured out as she returned the kiss with everything she had and more.

Two days later, rested and recovered from her ordeal, Meghan sat on the porch of her cottage waiting for Ryan. He'd called and told her that he was coming over. He'd sounded excited which made the waiting that much harder. They'd been inseparable for the past forty-eight hours except when he went home to sleep.

Each night Meghan dreamed of Ryan. Wonderful dreams full of what their life could be like. A house full of kids. Holidays spent together. Each morning she awoke anxious to see him.

She thanked God every moment for this second chance with Ryan. Only having Georgina in her arms would make her any happier.

Ryan's rig rolled down the street.

Anticipation and pleasure propelled her to her feet. She bounded down the walkway as he parked.

He stepped out of the driver's door. His expression brimmed with excitement. She flew into his arms. She would never tire of feeling his heart beat against hers.

"Come on," he said, tugging her around to the passenger side. He opened the door and flipped up the seat. Secured in a booster seat in the rear passenger seat was Georgina. Smiling, Georgina kicked her feet and raised her arms for Meghan.

Meghan let out a cry of pure joy. She hurriedly unbuckled the toddler and scooped her into her arms. Georgina clung to her. Meghan kissed her sweet blond head and chubby cheeks as tears of happiness ran down her face. Meghan turned her teary-eyed gaze to Ryan. "How?"

"Dad. He pulled some strings."

The hardness she had harbored toward Aiden softened. His kindness made her so happy.

"Is this just a visit?" she asked, barely daring to hope for more.

"Nope." The tender look in his eyes curled her toes. "You've been awarded temporary custody until permanent and full custody can be awarded."

Elated, Meghan held out her arm. Ryan stepped into her embrace. The three hugged in a tight clinch. They were a family. A bond that Meghan knew would never be broken.

EPILOGUE

Five months later

The back room at Connolly's Catch restaurant overflowed with excitement. Aiden Fitzgerald had been sworn in as mayor. The town had embraced Aiden, flaws and all. Just as she and Ryan had learned to do.

Ryan's arms went around Meghan and he planted a kiss on her lips. This was an important moment for Ryan, as well. He would be sworn in as chief of police in a few days.

She knew this was his dream, everything he wanted. Now if only her dreams could come true.

Outside the first of the season's nor'easters brought rain and wind to batter the windows. Enclosed inside the glass walls of the private room, Meghan held Ryan's hand tightly. She was so happy for Aiden. Over the past few months, she'd gotten to know Ryan's dad. He wasn't a bad man, just one who'd made mistakes. Like everyone else did at times. In fact, she'd found herself liking him. He was kind, and so loving to Georgina.

Georgina ran up and hugged her legs before taking off again to chase one of the other many young cousins. Meghan watched the toddler weave her way through the crowd totally comfortable with everyone. Affection and love made Meghan feel all gooey inside. She'd been awarded full custody of Georgina.

She and Georgina were gloriously happy living in the cottage on the beach. Ryan visited every day. Her relationship with him was deepening and growing. Meghan hoped that one day they'd make their own little family unit.

"This is so exciting," Merry said, placing her hand on her pregnant belly. "Even this little one is antsy tonight. Kicking up a storm."

Douglas put his arm around his wife. "He'll be a soccer player."

Merry arched an eyebrow. "Or she."

"Someone take these crab cakes," Keira said, holding the plate away from her recently wedded husband. "Nick doesn't need another one."

"Pass them this way." Charles reached for the plate.

"Hey, I'm not done with those," Nick protested with a mock pout.

Keira laughed and kissed her husband. "You gotta keep your girly figure."

"Ryan, rematch!" called Jamie Fitzgerald, setting his elbow on the edge of another table.

"Go on," Meghan urged. "Give the guy a break."

Ryan sauntered over, all swag and confidence, to arm wrestle his cousin. Meghan laughed.

"You're good for him," Fiona Fitzgerald said as she stepped up next to Meghan. Her engagement ring sparkled on her left hand. Meghan liked Ryan's red-haired sister. She was down-to-earth and had been a big help over the past few months when Meghan had parenting questions.

"I think we're good for each other," Meghan said, letting the revealing words slip out but knowing she was safe to do so with Fiona.

They shared a smile. Meghan hoped one day she'd be able to call this woman "sister."

The sound of metal against glass brought everyone's attention to the front of the room. Owen stood with his arms around Victoria and their daughter, Paige.

"Dad, as the newly elected mayor, would you perform your first official act and marry us?" Owen asked.

Cheers and sighs and clapping broke out. Aiden went to his youngest son and hugged him close. "Of course, son. If Victoria wants this."

"Sir, I've waited my whole life for this," Victoria replied with a wide smile.

Someone provided a Bible. Aiden officiated

their marriage, pronouncing the couple man and wife to the cheers of the family.

The election celebration turned into a wedding reception. Soon tables were moved aside and Aiden stood in for Victoria's deceased father and swirled her around the dance floor.

Georgina tugged at the hem of Meghan's sweater. She raised her chubby little arms indicting she wanted to be picked up. Meghan lifted her easily and set her on her hip. Georgina laid her head on Meghan's shoulder. Her eyelids drooped and she yawned, tired from playing with the other Fitzgerald and Connolly children.

"I'm going to take her home," she whispered to Ryan.

"Okay, let's go."

"You can stay," she said, not wanting to keep him from the celebration. "It's your family."

The look he gave had her pulse skittering. "This is *our* family."

She loved the sound of that.

"And they'll be fine without us," he said, guiding her toward the door.

When they returned to Meghan's cottage, Ryan followed her into the nursery where she laid Georgina on the gift Aiden had surprised her with one day—the toddler bed that had once belonged to Ryan and his siblings.

Georgina sighed and rolled over, her arm clutching a teddy bear.

Ryan took Meghan's hand. "She's so precious."

"She is," she agreed, liking the feeling of closeness, of connection she felt with him.

"Meghan," he said softly.

The note in his voice sent her heart pounding. He lifted her hand to his lips and kissed her knuckles. "I don't want this to ever end."

Breathless, she said, "What do you mean?"

"I mean, I want to stay here forever with you. You and Georgina. As a family. The three of us."

Tears of joy welled in her eyes. "Are you asking me to marry you?"

"Yes, if you'll have me."

She couldn't have asked for more. "Yes. Oh, yes." She threw her arms around his neck and kissed him with all the love and joy filling her heart.

"I think Georgina needs a sibling or two," Ryan said against her lips.

"I couldn't agree more." God willing, she wanted six little Fitzgeralds to shower with love.

* * * * *

Dear Reader,

I hope you enjoyed the final installment of the Fitzgerald Bay continuity series.

Faith and Family. That's the motto the Fitzgerald family has lived by for generations. An Irish family with a long history of public service made for a perfect setup for our heroes and heroines. The picturesque coastal fishing village north of Boston may have been fictional, but many times I found myself wishing I could visit and walk along the sandy shores of the bay.

Wrapping up a continuing suspense story is always challenging and I hope that the ending left you satisfied. The dedication and resolve of Ryan Fitzgerald and the spunk and determination of freelance journalist Meghan Henry, not only solved the murder of Olivia Henry, but also brought down a human-trafficking ring in the process.

The theme of forgiveness was woven through this story. Both Ryan and Meghan had to find the faith to forgive so they could be free to love. Something I know I struggle with in my life. But knowing that God forgave me helps me find the courage and the power to forgive others. I hope you find that same courage and power in God's love.

Coming in fall 2012, look for *The Doctor's*

Defender, the next Protection Specialists book in my own miniseries.

Until the next time we meet, may God keep you in His care.

Questions for Discussion

1. What made you pick up this book to read? In what ways did it live up to your expectations?

2. In what ways were Ryan and Meghan realistic characters? In what ways did their romance build believably?

3. If you read the first five books of the series, can you discuss the overarching suspense of Olivia's murder? Did you guess the culprit?

4. As Ryan and Meghan worked together to solve the murder, how did the suspense build?

5. What about the setting was clear and appealing? Could you envision Fitzgerald Bay?

6. Deputy Chief Ryan Fitzgerald was the eldest of six kids. He had a strong sense of responsibility. What role do you think birth order plays in the development of our personalities?

7. When Meghan Henry shed light on Aiden Fitzgerald's secret, Ryan reacted with anger and hurt and unforgiveness. What does God's word say about forgiveness?

8. Meghan counseled Ryan to forgive his father. What did forgiving his father do for Ryan? Can you tell of a time when you had to forgive someone? How did forgiving impact your life?

9. When Meghan Henry's cousin was murdered, Meghan relentlessly pushed to find the killer. Justice was important to Meghan. Can you discuss why justice is important? What does God's word say about justice?

10. Meghan learned that her cousin had had a child and wanted Meghan to raise her. Meghan faced many dangers, both physical and emotional, to gain custody of Georgina. If you were faced with a similar situation, how would you have proceeded? Was Meghan wise or reckless?

11. Ryan realized his own pride was keeping him from forgiving his father. How does pride block us from forgiveness? In what other ways is pride destructive?

12. Meghan yearned to belong. In what ways does a sense of belonging fulfill a need?

13. Ryan had three brothers and two sisters. Many cousins, aunts and uncles. To say the Fitzgeralds were a large family was an understate-

ment. What size family do you have? In what ways does your family stay connected?

14. Did you notice the scripture in the beginning of the book? What do you think God means by these words? What application does the scripture have to your life?

15. How did the author's use of language/writing style make this an enjoyable read?

16. What will be your most vivid memories of this book? What lessons about life, love and faith did you learn from this story?

LARGER-PRINT BOOKS!

**GET 2 FREE
LARGER-PRINT NOVELS
PLUS 2 FREE
MYSTERY GIFTS**

Love Inspired®
SUSPENSE
RIVETING INSPIRATIONAL ROMANCE

Larger-print novels are now available...

YES! Please send me 2 FREE LARGER-PRINT Love Inspired® Suspense novels and my 2 FREE mystery gifts (gifts are worth about $10). After receiving them, if I don't wish to receive any more books, I can return the shipping statement marked "cancel". If I don't cancel, I will receive 4 brand-new novels every month and be billed just $4.99 per book in the U.S. or $5.49 per book in Canada. That's a saving of at least 23% off the cover price. It's quite a bargain! Shipping and handling is just 50¢ per book in the U.S. and 75¢ per book in Canada.* I understand that accepting the 2 free books and gifts places me under no obligation to buy anything. I can always return a shipment and cancel at any time. Even if I never buy another book, the two free books and gifts are mine to keep forever.

110/310 IDN FEH3

Name	(PLEASE PRINT)	
Address		Apt. #
City	State/Prov.	Zip/Postal Code

Signature (if under 18, a parent or guardian must sign)

Mail to the **Reader Service:**
IN U.S.A.: P.O. Box 1867, Buffalo, NY 14240-1867
IN CANADA: P.O. Box 609, Fort Erie, Ontario L2A 5X3

Not valid for current subscribers to Love Inspired Suspense larger-print books.

**Are you a current subscriber to Love Inspired Suspense books
and want to receive the larger-print edition?
Call 1-800-873-8635 or visit www.ReaderService.com.**

* Terms and prices subject to change without notice. Prices do not include applicable taxes. Sales tax applicable in N.Y. Canadian residents will be charged applicable taxes. Offer not valid in Quebec. This offer is limited to one order per household. All orders subject to credit approval. Credit or debit balances in a customer's account(s) may be offset by any other outstanding balance owed by or to the customer. Please allow 4 to 6 weeks for delivery. Offer available while quantities last.

Your Privacy—The Reader Service is committed to protecting your privacy. Our Privacy Policy is available online at www.ReaderService.com or upon request from the Reader Service.

We make a portion of our mailing list available to reputable third parties that offer products we believe may interest you. If you prefer that we not exchange your name with third parties, or if you wish to clarify or modify your communication preferences, please visit us at www.ReaderService.com/consumerschoice or write to us at Reader Service Preference Service, P.O. Box 9062, Buffalo, NY 14269. Include your complete name and address.

LISUSLP11B

LARGER-PRINT BOOKS!

GET 2 FREE LARGER-PRINT NOVELS PLUS 2 FREE MYSTERY GIFTS

Love Inspired®

Larger-print novels are now available...

YES! Please send me 2 FREE LARGER-PRINT Love Inspired® novels and my 2 FREE mystery gifts (gifts are worth about $10). After receiving them, if I don't wish to receive any more books, I can return the shipping statement marked "cancel". If I don't cancel, I will receive 6 brand-new novels every month and be billed just $4.99 per book in the U.S. or $5.49 per book in Canada. That's a saving of at least 23% off the cover price. It's quite a bargain! Shipping and handling is just 50¢ per book in the U.S. and 75¢ per book in Canada.* I understand that accepting the 2 free books and gifts places me under no obligation to buy anything. I can always return a shipment and cancel at any time. Even if I never buy another book, the two free books and gifts are mine to keep forever.

122/322 IDN FEG3

Name	(PLEASE PRINT)	
Address		Apt. #
City	State/Prov.	Zip/Postal Code

Signature (if under 18, a parent or guardian must sign)

Mail to the Reader Service:
IN U.S.A.: P.O. Box 1867, Buffalo, NY 14240-1867
IN CANADA: P.O. Box 609, Fort Erie, Ontario L2A 5X3

Not valid to current subscribers to Love Inspired Larger-print books.

Are you a current subscriber to Love Inspired books and want to receive the larger-print edition? Call 1-800-873-8635 or visit www.ReaderService.com.

* Terms and prices subject to change without notice. Prices do not include applicable taxes. Sales tax applicable in N.Y. Canadian residents will be charged applicable taxes. Offer not valid in Quebec. This offer is limited to one order per household. All orders subject to credit approval. Credit or debit balances in a customer's account(s) may be offset by any other outstanding balance owed by or to the customer. Please allow 4 to 6 weeks for delivery. Offer available while quantities last.

Your Privacy—The Reader Service is committed to protecting your privacy. Our Privacy Policy is available online at www.ReaderService.com or upon request from the Reader Service.

We make a portion of our mailing list available to reputable third parties that offer products we believe may interest you. If you prefer that we not exchange your name with third parties, or if you wish to clarify or modify your communication preferences, please visit us at www.ReaderService.com/consumerchoice or write to us at Reader Service Preference Service, P.O. Box 9062, Buffalo, NY 14269. Include your complete name and address.

LILPI1B

ReaderService.com

You can now manage your account online!

- Review your order history
- Manage your payments
- Update your address

We've redesigned the Reader Service website just for you.

Now you can:

- Read excerpts
- Respond to mailings and special monthly offers
- Learn about new series available to you

Visit us today:

www.ReaderService.com

RS10